I Can See You

Nick Shadow

A division of Hachette Children's Books

Special thanks to Shaun Hutson

For Matt Haslum, for all his hard work in adding books to the Library

Created by Working Partners Limited, London W6 0QT

First published in Great Britain in 2006
by Hodder Children's Books

1

A Catalogue record for this book is available from the British Library

ISBN-10: 0 340 93021 7
ISBN-13: 978 0 340 93021 2

Typeset in Weiss by Avon DataSet Ltd,
Bidford-on-Avon, Warwickshire

Printed and bound in Great Britain by
Clays Ltd, St Ives plc

The paper and board used in this paperback by Hodder Children's Books are natural recyclable products made from wood grown in sustainable forests. The manufacturing processes conform to the environmental regulations of the country of origin.

Hodder Children's Books
A division of Hachette Children's Books
338 Euston Road
London NW1 3BH

Welcome, reader.

My name is Nick Shadow,
curator of that secret
institution:

The Midnight Library

Where is the Midnight Library, you ask?
Why have you never heard of it?
For the sake of your own safety, these questions are better left unanswered. However ... so long as you promise not to reveal where you heard the following (no matter who or *what* demands it of you), I will reveal what I keep here in the ancient vaults.
After many years of searching, I have gathered the most terrifying collection of stories known to man. They will chill you to your very core, and make flesh creep on your young, brittle bones. Perhaps you should summon up the courage and turn the page. After all, what's the worst that could happen ... ?

The Midnight Library: Volume VII

Stories by Shaun Hutson

CONTENTS

I CAN SEE YOU

Where is everyone? Michael Lewis wondered as he cycled along the road. He'd left his new home, Axby Farm, on his way to school nearly ten minutes ago, but during that time he'd seen only one vehicle on the road. A tractor had pulled out from a dirt track on to one of the narrow country thoroughfares that snaked through the fields and hills around the farm. Other than that, Michael hadn't seen so much as another bike since he'd set off.

The contrast with his journey to school in London couldn't have been more obvious. Back there he spent most of the ride dodging cars, buses and taxis. Out here, it seemed, he had the road to himself.

Perhaps, he thought, no one left their homes on a Monday morning out here in the countryside. He was still thinking about that when he swung his bike around a sharp bend and saw a car coming the other way. Michael smiled, almost relieved to see that someone other than himself was on the move.

The driver of the car waved happily at Michael as he passed and Michael nodded back, remembering that the tractor driver he'd seen had also waved. People were certainly friendly here. As he cycled on he glanced to his left and saw a horse peering over the hedge at him. Michael grinned at the watching animal, wondering whether it was going to wave at him too.

Still smiling broadly, he guided his bike around

another bend in the road and down a steep hill towards Beech Hill School. As he drew nearer, Michael could see the red brick buildings and pupils moving around in the playground and on the sports field. Some were in groups, others wandered about in pairs. It didn't look as though anyone was on their own.

Michael felt a pang of nervousness as he realized that he wasn't going to know anyone. Still, the friendly waves he'd received on the way to school had to be a good sign, he figured. Hopefully the kids would be friendly too.

He brought his bike to a halt, noting that several of the other pupils were eyeing him with curiosity. Michael chained his bike to the metal rack in the playground, hoisted his rucksack on to his back and wandered across the tarmac, looking around. Away to his right, some boys were playing a noisy game of football. To his left, three girls stared at him and giggled as he passed. He headed for the school playing-field, feeling more than a little nervous at the prospect of his first day in his new school.

Then, suddenly, a tennis ball landed at his feet. Michael looked up to see where it had come from.

'Over here,' a voice called and he turned round to see a tall lad jogging towards him, followed by a group of shorter boys.

Michael stooped to retrieve the tennis ball and throw it back but, by that time, the little group was right next to him. The tall boy held out his hand and Michael dropped the tennis ball into his outstretched palm.

'You're new, aren't you?' one of the other boys said.

Michael nodded. 'Yes,' he said, smiling. 'My name's Michael.'

'Where did you live before you moved here?' another asked.

'London,' Michael told him.

'You're living at Axby Farm, aren't you?' the first boy went on.

Michael nodded again.

'So where did you park your bulldozer?' The question had come from the tallest of the boys. 'That's why you and your family are here, isn't it?' he continued coldly. 'To flatten the countryside and build a shopping centre?'

'No,' Michael said. It was true that his father was a property developer, and, in fact, Michael knew he had bought Axby Farm with the original intention of developing a shopping mall on the site. But then he'd fallen in love with the place and decided to move the whole family in instead. The shopping mall plan was well and truly shelved. 'But it might not be a bad idea,' Michael added, jokingly. 'It looks as if you could use one out here.'

This did not go down well. The tall boy took an angry step towards Michael, who wondered if he was about to create some kind of world record for getting into a fight quicker than anyone else ever had on their first day at a new school.

In fact, the boy prodded Michael in the chest with one finger. 'See you later, city boy,' he said. Then he turned and strode away, the others bounding along behind him like hyenas following a lion.

Michael breathed a sigh of relief.

'I don't think the joke about the shopping centre was such a good idea, do you?' said a voice nearby. 'It *was* a joke, wasn't it?'

'Yes,' Michael replied, turning to see a girl with long, tangled hair and a broad grin.

'Don't worry about them,' she advised. 'They'll get over it.'

'Thanks for that,' Michael said. 'I was worrying a bit.'

'Andrew Scutt can be a bully,' she continued. 'He's the tall one. The others are like his posse, but they're OK when Andrew's not around.'

'Posse. Now that's not a word I expected to hear outside the city,' Michael laughed.

'Just because we live in the country doesn't mean

we're backward, you know,' the girl said, smiling at him. 'My name's Stephanie, by the way. You're Michael, aren't you? Miss Hamilton told us last week you'd be joining our class.'

'Did she tell you my dad was going to bulldoze all your houses and build a shopping mall out here too?' Michael wanted to know. 'Is that why King Kong over there was waiting for me?'

Stephanie laughed and shook her head. 'There have been stories and speculation in the local paper for months about a developer buying up land for a shopping centre,' she explained. 'People round here aren't too keen on the idea. They figure we've managed this long without one, we don't need one now.'

'So where do you go shopping?' Michael asked.

'There are shops and a market in the village,' Stephanie replied. 'And more shops in Wakely – that's about seven miles from here. There's a cinema there too if you need something to do.'

'I've got plenty to do at the moment helping my

mum and dad clean up the farm,' Michael said. He grinned ruefully. 'Unfortunately.'

'So your family's moved into Axby Farm, huh?'

'Did your teacher tell you that as well?' Michael asked.

'No, my dad did. And it was reported in the local paper that Axby Farm had been sold,' Stephanie told him.

'Do they report on every house that's sold?'

'No. But no one's lived at Axby Farm for years! Everyone thought it was going to be there that the shopping centre was built. I think most people were relieved when they heard that a family had moved in.'

'Everyone except Andrew over there,' Michael murmured.

'I told you,' Stephanie said. 'Ignore him. Not all of us are like that.'

'I'm glad you're not,' he grinned. 'I was wondering when I was going to see a friendly face.'

Stephanie smiled back and motioned for him to

follow her as the school bell sounded for the beginning of lessons. 'I'll show you where Miss Hamilton's classroom is,' she told him. 'And I promise not to chew hay or talk about pig breeding all through today's lessons, OK?'

'Cool,' Michael said, laughing as he followed her through the main doors into school.

Michael put down his pen and looked around the classroom. He felt less nervous now, despite his potentially hazardous start to the day. He glanced across at Stephanie. She had really helped him settle into his new school. His new teacher had turned out to be nice too, and the essay on Amazon rainforests that she had given the class to write wasn't difficult. In fact, Michael found that he'd finished before most of the others.

He sat back and looked around the room. At the desk next to him, Stephanie was still writing, stopping occasionally to consult her textbook.

Miss Hamilton got up from her desk. 'Just

carry on working,' she said. 'I've got to fetch some books from the school library. I'll be back in a few minutes.' She left, closing the door behind her.

A vague murmur of chatter arose from the class. Michael grinned: this wasn't like his school back in London. If a teacher left her class there, the whole place immediately erupted with shouting and laughing. Obviously, Michael decided, his new schoolmates were better behaved. He listened to a couple of boys in front of him telling another about their fishing expedition of the previous weekend.

'Yeah, it was great,' one boy was saying. 'I got a perch and Tom caught some sticklebacks.'

Fishing? Sitting beside some water with a worm on a hook, trying to catch fish, didn't sound very exciting to Michael. *Is that their idea of fun?* he wondered. *Perhaps they watch cows grazing when they want something really exciting to do!*

He was relieved when lunch-time finally arrived

and he, like the rest of the school, trooped out to the playground again.

'Come on, city boy,' Stephanie said, coming up behind Michael and tugging his arm. 'You can sit with me for lunch.'

Michael nodded and followed her round to the steps of the main building. They both sat down and pulled their lunch boxes out of their rucksacks. Michael tucked into his sandwich and gazed around the playground.

'Having fun?' Stephanie asked.

'Do you ever get bored living in the country?' Michael countered.

'Why should I? There's plenty to do.'

'Like what? Fishing?' he asked. 'Walking? When I go out, I see fields. That's it, just fields and nothing else. Back home, I could kick a football against a wall. Here, if I kick a ball I end up chasing after it for miles – and stepping in about ten cowpats on the way!'

Stephanie laughed. 'Sorry, Michael,' she said

smiling. 'It's going to take you a while to get used to living around here, that's all. What would you have done back in the city?'

Michael shrugged. 'I don't know – loads of things. We'd go to the cinema, or bowling, or to McDonald's. There was just so much more to do.'

'You can do all those things here too, you know,' Stephanie told him. 'All you have to do is get on a bus first. It's not such a big deal. You're not telling me everything was within two minutes' walk of your house when you lived in London, are you?'

Michael shook his head. 'No, it wasn't, you're right,' he conceded. 'So what do you do at the weekends?'

'I go and see my friends, play with my little brother, listen to my iPod, stuff like that.'

'You have an iPod?'

'And an X-Box. And a DVD player. We've even got running water, you know,' Stephanie said, laughing.

'I know that,' Michael grunted as she punched

him playfully on the arm. 'I just had the wrong impression of the country and the people who live here. Sorry.'

'Don't worry about it,' she told him. 'In another six months you'll have forgotten you ever lived anywhere else!'

'Yeah, you never know, I might even take up fishing,' Michael said, grinning.

As Michael trudged along through the fields, he looked at the shopping list his mum had given him and couldn't help but wonder what his mates back in London were doing this Saturday morning. *Probably still in bed*, he thought, since it was barely nine o'clock.

He was pretty sure that none of them would be out on an errand for their mum. Even if they were, it wouldn't involve a long walk in to some village market to buy fresh fruit. Michael shook his head. His mum had decided that she wanted to make jam! She'd never made jam in her life before they'd moved to Axby Farm. His parents were getting into the country life in a big way!

Michael stuck his hand into his pocket and pulled out his mobile phone. He hadn't been able to get a signal anywhere since they'd moved into the farm, but now, as he stood on one of the hills that overlooked the farmhouse, he wondered if the reception might be better.

He dialled his friend, Matt, and waited hopefully. When the word 'Calling' appeared on the screen, Michael nearly shouted for joy. Instead, he pressed the phone to his ear.

'Hello,' said a familiar voice.

'Matt,' said Michael, excitedly. 'It's me, Mike Lewis.'

'Mike!' Matt exclaimed. 'Hello, mate, I . . . ever . . . you . . .' His voice was cutting in and out, making it hard for Michael to make head or tail of what he was saying.

'Matt, can you hear me?' Michael shouted into the phone. There was no reply. Michael cursed and scrambled further up the hill in hopes of getting better reception.

'Matt, are you still there?' he tried again.

Silence.

Michael took the phone away from his ear to look at the screen. It was displaying the operator's logo. It had disconnected. And now the signal strength was weak. He sighed and shoved the mobile back into his pocket.

He looked around to see that he was now up to his waist in tall, waving grass. He'd been so intent on his attempts to reach his friend that he hadn't noticed he'd strayed off the footpath. He forged ahead towards a line of trees at the top of the hill, feeling like an explorer making his way through the jungle.

When he finally reached the hilltop, he was impressed by the view. Looking back the way he'd come, Michael could see the whole of Axby Farm spread out below him. The farmhouse itself nestled in the valley at the base of the hill he was standing on and slightly to his right. About half a mile in front of the farmhouse, stretching away to his left, was a large beech forest. And on the far side of the farmhouse was another hill, topped by a single towering oak tree.

Michael turned to look at the view in the other direction. At the base of the hill, a small river curled away like a silver ribbon. He remembered his father saying that it was called Beech Rill and that it formed the western boundary of Axby Farm. A wooden bridge led across the river towards a tiny church. And on the other side of that was the village to which he was headed.

Michael ran down the hill and over the bridge to the churchyard. He had no idea how old the church itself was but, from the look of its weather-beaten stonework, he guessed it had to be at least four or five hundred years old – possibly more. The churchyard was surrounded by a low stone wall that he was just about to clamber over when he noticed a wooden gate that led inside.

He hurried over to the gate and walked in. The graveyard was tangled and overgrown, the headstones crumbling like rotten teeth. Many were tilted at impossible angles and some had fallen over long since and were now covered in moss. Michael moved close to one and tried to read the inscription on the weathered stone.

'Frances Hutchens,' he murmured. 'Born 1745. Died 1801.'

He moved on to the next headstone. He couldn't make out the name but the date of the occupant's death was visible as 1789.

'What are you doing?' hissed a voice suddenly.

Michael spun round in surprise, his heart hammering against his ribs, and promptly tripped over a gravestone. He went flying to the ground, landing with a thud in the long grass. From his new position, he could see Stephanie peeping out from behind a tombstone.

'Stephanie!' Michael exclaimed, struggling to his

feet. 'You scared the hell out of me. What are you doing?'

'I'm playing hide and seek with my little brother,' Stephanie told him, grabbing his sweatshirt and pulling him down into the grass again. 'Now keep quiet or he'll hear us.'

Michael nodded and moved further behind the gravestone with Stephanie.

'What were *you* doing anyway?' Stephanie continued, lowering her voice.

'I just stopped to read the gravestones. I'm on my way to the market to get some stuff for my mum,' Michael explained. 'By the way, I tried to call one of my mates—'

'Shhhh!' Stephanie interrupted, pressing a finger to her lips. 'I told you, I don't want Jack to find me. You can play too if you like.'

'Wow, thanks!' Michael said, trying to sound enthusiastic.

'Well, would you rather be shopping for your mum?' Stephanie asked.

'Yeah, all right then, point taken,' Michael said, grinning and lowering his voice. 'I can't get a decent signal on my mobile round here,' he went on, 'which is really annoying because I want to call one of my mates back in London.'

'Do you want to tell him about your new home?' Stephanie smiled. 'Are you going to mention that you nearly woke Farmer Axby?'

Michael looked puzzled, and Stephanie nodded in the direction of the gravestone he'd tripped over.

'"George Joseph Axby",' Michael read. '"Born 1863. Died 1907. May He Find Peace in Death." This is Farmer Axby's grave!'

'Yup, the grave of the man whose house you're living in,' Stephanie told him. 'Haven't you heard the story of Farmer Axby? It's well known around here.'

'I thought no one had lived at Axby Farm for about a hundred years,' Michael said.

'They haven't,' Stephanie confirmed. 'Not properly. Farmer Axby and his family were the last ones. Other people have tried to move in over the years, but they've never stayed. They say that strange lights in the night and the smell of burning flesh has driven everyone away. Noticed anything like that since you moved in?' she asked brightly.

Michael shook his head. 'No, and I hope I don't!' he said with feeling. 'So, go on, what happened to Farmer Axby?'

'Well, he was a mean, grumpy old man,' Stephanie explained, 'but he got even worse when his wife left him, taking his two children with her. According to local legend,' she went on, warming to her tale, 'Farmer Axby used to sit at his bedroom window every night just staring into the darkness, waiting for his family to come back. Sitting there all those nights drove him mad, and he started imagining that he could actually *see* his wife and children coming back to him across the fields. One night, he was so sure he'd seen them that he grabbed a lantern and rushed outside. He ran backwards and forwards in the darkness calling out "I can see you", but he couldn't, of course, because they weren't there. He was out there for hours, shouting and screaming. Finally he must have stumbled and dropped the lantern, because it smashed and set fire to his coat. He was burned alive.'

Michael swallowed hard.

'They say he was still screaming "I can see you" while he was burning,' Stephanie said with a shudder. 'And some people say that, on certain nights, you can still smell his burning flesh on the hills where he died.'

'Yeah, right,' Michael said, dismissively.

Stephanie shrugged. 'I'm only telling you the story,' she said.

Michael frowned then shook his head. 'It's just some local superstition,' he grunted.

'Maybe,' she mused. 'But you'd better not upset Farmer Axby. You don't want him to come looking for you, city boy.'

'Very funny, Stephanie,' Michael said, rolling his

eyes. But he looked warily at the gravestone that had tripped him up.

'Got you!' declared a triumphant voice, making them both jump.

Michael got to his feet and turned to see a smiling little boy with bright red hair standing behind him.

'Jack,' Stephanie laughed, getting up too.

'I knew . . . I'd find . . . you,' the little lad said breathlessly. He looked curiously at Michael.

'Michael, this is my brother,' Stephanie announced, pointing at the boy who was now reaching inside his jeans for what Michael saw was an inhaler. 'Jack, this is Michael, the new boy.'

'I've got asthma,' Jack said, almost proudly, taking a pull on the inhaler.

Michael nodded.

'It's my turn to hide now,' Jack said, bouncing up and down.

'Do you want to stay and play with us?' Stephanie asked.

'No, thanks,' Michael said. 'I'd better get to the market and collect that stuff for my mum. Next time I'll stay,' he promised.

'Are you going to play "I Can See You"?' Jack demanded, as Michael was about to leave.

Michael turned back, looking puzzled.

'It's a version of hide and seek,' Stephanie explained. 'We all play – all the kids from the village. Every September 22nd, the anniversary of Farmer Axby's death, we come out into the fields around Axby Farm after dark and try to find each other. It's a good laugh. It might be good for you to play, Michael. It'll get you involved with some of the others from school. If they see you joining in with one of our games they might not think of you as so much of an outsider.'

Michael nodded. 'September 22nd?' he muttered. 'That's tomorrow night.'

'Are you up for it, then?' Stephanie asked. 'It's even more special this year because it's the hundredth anniversary of Farmer Axby's death.'

'All right then,' Michael agreed, nodding.

'Jack and I will call for you at eight.'

'OK,' Michael said happily, making his way out of the graveyard.

'And Michael,' Stephanie called, 'don't forget your torch.'

'The others have been talking about it at school, Dad,' Michael said, taking another mouthful of his dinner. From his seat at the table in the cosy farmhouse kitchen, Michael glanced at the window. It was dark outside and a harsh wind had picked up, whipping across the fields and whistling around the house itself until the windows rattled in their frames.

'It must be a big thing round here,' his mum offered. 'When I drove into the village this afternoon the lady who runs the post office mentioned it. Her daughter's playing. It seems as if the whole village look on it as some kind of special event.'

'They do,' Michael enthused. 'Is it all right if I join in?'

'I don't see why not,' his dad remarked.

'It just seems a bit bizarre, playing a game to *celebrate* someone's death,' his mum commented. 'Besides, are you sure you want to be wandering about in those fields at all hours of the night?'

'Sure,' Michael said. 'Anyway, it's not celebrating Farmer Axby's death. It's just the locals' way of remembering what happened. And you don't have to worry about me, Mum. I'm thirteen, you know, not six. Besides, you were the ones who said I should get involved in local things.'

'As a matter of fact, I was talking to Stephanie's dad about it today,' Mr Lewis put in. 'He wanted to warn me that tomorrow night we're going to have most of the kids from the village running across our land, trying to find each other in the dark. He said he used to play himself when he was a kid. I don't think there's any harm in it.'

Michael nodded. 'It's only a game,' he said,

finishing his dinner and pushing the plate away.

The wind screamed around the house again. Outside in the yard, the door of the barn swung open on its creaky hinges and then slammed shut with a bang.

'Oh, where is it?' Michael muttered irritably as he rummaged in another of the boxes of belongings stacked up in his bedroom, searching desperately for something that didn't seem to be there.

'What are you looking for, Mike?'

He turned to see his mum standing in the doorway peering in at him.

'A torch,' Michael told her. 'Stephanie and Jack'll be here in ten minutes and I can't find a torch. I can't play "I Can See You" without a torch, can I?'

'Your dad's got one downstairs,' his mum told him. 'Use that for tonight.'

Michael hurried out of the room and down to the kitchen.

'Dad,' he shouted excitedly. 'Where's the torch? Can I borrow it for the game?'

'In the drawer next to the cooker,' his dad shouted from the living-room.

Michael found it immediately and flicked it on, pleased to see that it gave off a broad, bright beam.

'Are you all ready now?' his dad said, entering the kitchen.

'Yes, I'm just waiting for Stephanie and Jack.'

As if in response to Michael's words, there was a knock at the front door and his dad headed off to answer it.

Seconds later, Stephanie and Jack wandered into the kitchen, both dressed in thick coats, hats, scarves and gloves. Stephanie carried a torch as well which she shone at Michael, laughing.

'Are you ready to go?' she asked.

Michael nodded, threw on his coat and they all headed out of the front door.

'Just make sure you look after him, will you,

Stephanie?' Michael's dad said, grinning. 'I don't want him getting lost in the dark.'

'Dad,' Michael said through clenched teeth, 'I'll be fine.'

'I'll take care of him, Mr Lewis,' Stephanie smiled. 'Don't worry.'

Then the trio headed out across the windy farmyard while Michael's dad waved cheerily from the warmth of the house.

'Why do parents have to be so embarrassing?' Michael muttered as he strode along.

'They can't help it,' Stephanie said, grinning. 'It's in their genes.'

The three of them made their way down the dirt track that led from Axby Farm into the surrounding fields. Michael was struck by how dark the night truly was when there were no streetlights to break it up. More than once he stumbled on the uneven ground, barely able to see more than an arm's length in front of him.

'It's a good job there's no moon tonight,'

Stephanie said. 'That'll make the game even more exciting.'

'I know,' Michael muttered, 'but if there was a moon, at least we'd be able to see where we're going. I can hardly see a thing!' He flicked on his torch, the beam cutting through the darkness.

'Don't put that on yet,' Stephanie told him.

'But we can walk faster when we can see the way,' Michael protested.

'Yes, but if you keep it switched off, your eyes will get used to the dark and then you will be able to see perfectly well,' Stephanie explained patiently. 'Trust me.'

Michael nodded and switched the torch off again, trailing along behind Stephanie and Jack who moved through the gloom and over the uneven land as easily as if they had night-vision goggles on.

They all climbed a low hill, the tall grass whipping at their legs as the wind caught it, and Michael heard a strange clattering sound not too far ahead. Peering through the darkness, he realized that it was the sound of the wind rattling the branches of the large oak tree that he had seen at the top of the hill when he had gazed out over the farm in daylight.

Michael was so busy staring at the oak tree that he almost tripped. He looked down to see what he had blundered into in the blackness, but it was impossible to make out amid the long grass. As he raised his head, the blinding white glare of a torch beam made him wince. The light was being shone directly into his eyes.

'I didn't expect to see you tonight, city boy,' said an all-too-familiar voice. It was Andrew Scutt. He kept the torch trained on Michael's face as he spoke.

Michael pulled his own torch from his pocket and shone it back at Andrew, who waited a moment then switched his off.

In the light of his own torch, Michael could see more of his schoolmates and also several others from the village that he didn't recognize. He guessed there must have been nearly thirty of them gathered on the overgrown slope, standing in a semicircle. He kept his torch levelled at Andrew for a moment longer, then switched it off when the beam flickered slightly.

'Listen, everybody,' Andrew said, raising his voice to make himself heard above the howling wind. 'It's September 22nd, and you all know what that means . . .'

Some of the waiting group clapped and cheered.

'I think most of you have played before, but I'll explain the rules again anyway,' he continued, looking in Michael's direction. 'When I give the signal, we all split up and everyone has ten minutes to find a good starting place. But you've got to stick to the land around Axby Farm, right? So that means, no further than the woods to the north, this hill to the east, Beech Rill to the west and the main road to the south.'

There were murmurs of approval from the others.

'After ten minutes, we all start looking for each other in the dark,' Andrew went on. 'When you think you've found another player, you flash your torch at them and call out "I Can See You", same as old Farmer Axby did all those years ago. Then you say the name of the person you've seen. Understand?'

The others watching and listening nodded or muttered in agreement.

'The person who's been spotted must then stand still, with their torch switched on and shining at themselves, like this, to show that they're out of the game,' Andrew explained. To illustrate his point, he flicked his own torch on and shone it upwards from beneath his chin, momentarily illuminating his face. 'The last player to remain unseen is the winner. Now, before we start, everyone check the batteries in their torch.'

All over the hillside, beams of light cut through the blackness as the others did as they were instructed. Michael flicked on his own torch, muttering to himself as the beam faded and then went out completely. He pressed the ON/OFF switch again. This time the light shone brightly for a couple of seconds but then turned to a weak yellow glow and died.

'You should have checked those batteries before you left home, city boy,' Andrew Scutt laughed smugly, throwing his own shiny red torch into the air and catching it again. Michael noticed that it looked brand-new – no risk of Andrew's torch running out of battery power!

'You can't play "I Can See You" when you can't see anyone, can you? It looks like you're out of the game. What a shame,' sneered Andrew.

'It was fine earlier,' Michael said irritably.

'It's no problem,' Stephanie said, stepping closer. 'You can team up with Jack and me.'

'Do you mind?' Michael said, feeling sheepish.

She smiled and shook her head.

'Right, so Stephanie's going to baby-sit the city boy,' scoffed Andrew. 'You've already got your little brother with you, you know,' he reminded her. 'If there's three of you together, you've got no chance. You'll be spotted straight away!'

'That's my problem,' Stephanie said. 'We'll still last longer than you, Andrew.'

'We'll see,' the big lad said, smirking. 'Right,' he called. 'Check your watches. You've got ten minutes to find your starting places!'

Stephanie grabbed Michael's arm and tugged him away with her and Jack as all the others on the hillside also hurried away into the gloom.

'Stay close to me,' Stephanie whispered. 'We'll head round behind the big oak tree. There's an old, dried up stream bed near there where we can hide.'

Michael had to strain his ears to hear her over the gusts of strong wind. He was careful to stay close to Stephanie and Jack so that he could keep them in sight. With all the torches off, the night had closed in again, darker than ever, and though Michael could hear footsteps moving hurriedly in all directions, he could see no one but his own little group.

'I hope you know where you're going,' Michael whispered after a moment.

'Shhhhh,' Stephanie hissed at him over her shoulder, her breath clouding in the cold night air. 'I know *exactly* where I'm going.'

Michael shrugged and hurried after her through the darkness.

Suddenly, he almost fell over. His left foot had connected with what he could only imagine was a tree-stump or a rock. It took all his efforts to remain upright.

He peered ahead through the gloom and saw that Stephanie and Jack had clambered over a fallen tree and dropped into what looked like a shallow trench. Michael carefully scrambled over the tree-trunk too and crouched down beside Stephanie.

'This is the old stream bed,' she told him quietly. 'It leads all the way from here across Axby Farm, as far as the woods to the north. It's a great way of getting around without the others seeing us. Even if they think they've heard something and they shine their torches this way, we only have to duck down and the beams will go right over our heads!'

'Cool!' said Jack, wheezing a little.

'Are you OK, Jack?' Stephanie asked. 'The cold air makes your asthma worse, doesn't it?'

'I'm fine,' Jack told her, waving his inhaler reassuringly under her nose.

'Right,' said Stephanie, checking her watch. 'This will be our starting place. The ten minutes are almost up. Everyone else will be on the move soon, looking for each other. So let's get going.' She began to edge along the dry stream bed followed by her little brother. Michael brought up the rear.

Michael walked as quickly and quietly as he could manage, but the stream bed was full of dry leaves that rustled underfoot. Suddenly there was a sharp *crack* as he stepped on a fallen twig.

Jack whipped round and Stephanie glared at

him. Michael grimaced and mouthed 'Sorry' in the darkness. Then he looked around anxiously in case the sound had alerted anyone close at hand. The branches of the nearby oak tree rattled noisily as the wind continued to blow. Michael heaved a sigh of relief, and hoped that the noise would distract anyone listening.

'Come on,' Stephanie whispered. 'We need to keep moving.'

The trio crept on. Michael scanned the ground before him carefully this time to make sure he didn't step on anything else that could give their position away. He wondered where all the others were hiding.

Then he saw a shape move high up on the hillside. He was just about to touch Stephanie's shoulder and point it out to her when he realized that what he was looking at wasn't human. It moved like a fox, but it was really big, *too* big to be a fox, Michael decided. It had to be a stray dog.

He returned his attention to the game and

scanned the area for other players. Up ahead, about a hundred metres away, he thought he could see the shadowy outlines of some of the others but, as he, Stephanie and Jack drew closer, Michael saw that the shapes were merely bushes, buffeted by the strong wind.

He realized he'd been holding his breath, so he let it out slowly and was just beginning to relax when he saw a bright beam of light cut through the night away to his right.

'Get down!' Michael hissed urgently, and Stephanie and Jack dropped to their knees. Then they all peered over the edge of the stream bed, trying to see whether someone was illuminated in the torchlight.

'Look, someone's been found,' Jack said quietly, pointing to a girl who was standing holding her torch beam under her chin.

'It's Simone,' Stephanie chuckled. 'I should have known; she's always the first to get caught.' She turned to look at Jack and Michael. 'We'll go and hide down by the old gate near the bottom of the hill for a while. This stream bed will take us right to it.'

'I thought the idea was to find people,' Michael pointed out.

'It is,' Stephanie agreed. 'But there's an old dirt track that runs through the gate and loads of people use it. If we hide down there we can catch people as they come by.'

Michael grinned. 'Good plan,' he said approvingly.

As Stephanie and Jack set off, Michael glanced back for Simone, lit up by the torchlight. But, to his surprise, he saw nothing but darkness. No light. No figure. Nothing. Simone was no longer there.

Michael shrugged, wondering if her torch batteries had died like his own. Then he followed after Jack and Stephanie, pulling up the collar of his coat and shivering. The night seemed to be growing ever colder. The wind that had been blowing so ferociously at the start of the game had eased slightly now but, in its place, a freezing fog was beginning to form on the ground, swirling around Michael's legs in wispy clouds.

Just as Michael caught up with his friends, he heard movement nearby. It was definitely the sound of footsteps, and he could hear breathing too. There was someone within metres of them.

Quickly, he gestured to Stephanie and Jack and all three of them froze, crouching low to the ground. Michael waited for the torch beam to shine on them, certain that whoever was nearby must have heard them, but no light broke the darkness, although Michael could still hear breathing. He guessed that the person must be getting their breath back while they scanned the dark hillside for fellow competitors.

Stephanie reached back and tapped Michael on the shoulder, then touched her torch. Clearly she too had heard the breathing and planned to catch the other person with the light from her torch. But she hesitated and Michael could see that she was listening carefully, presumably wanting to be sure of where the person was.

Eventually Stephanie smiled at Michael and nodded. She held up one finger, then two, then three. As she raised the third, she, Michael and Jack sprang up from their hiding-place, and Stephanie shone the torch in the direction of the breathing.

'I can see you, Jacob Niles,' Stephanie yelled gleefully as the torch beam cast brilliant white light on the figure of a boy standing with his back to them.

The boy gasped in surprise and whirled around to face them. 'Oh, no,' he groaned, caught in the beam of the torch like a startled rabbit.

Michael, Stephanie and Jack laughed.

'Put your torch on, Jacob,' Stephanie told him. 'You're out.'

Jacob nodded, switched on his own torch and shone it under his chin. 'I never even saw you,' he moaned, shaking his head.

'That's the whole idea,' Stephanie chuckled,

switching off her own torch. 'Now don't tell anyone which direction we went, will you?'

Jacob shook his head sullenly, watching as the three of them crawled away in the darkness and the fog, hidden from view even more effectively by the bank of the ditch they were in.

Michael was smiling broadly as he, Stephanie and Jack continued on their way. He was really beginning to enjoy the game, and he was suddenly curious as to how many other people had been found. He paused and peered cautiously up over the lip of the ditch. Scattered across the fields, he could see the light from various torches, indicating that others had been caught. At least ten, he figured, counting the lights quickly.

Stephanie had been right. It was a good game, and the fact that they'd managed to stay undiscovered for what seemed like ages was making him feel even better. The prospect of winning really added to the excitement and he wondered what

Andrew Scutt would say at the end of the game if he got beaten by the 'city boy'. Michael crossed his fingers in the dark. He couldn't wait.

Unfortunately, he was so wrapped up in his thoughts of victory that he slipped on some fallen leaves and bumped into Stephanie, who promptly dropped the torch. It rolled away into the darkness.

Michael was about to scramble to his feet when Stephanie waved a hand frantically to indicate that he should stay down.

'There's someone there,' Stephanie breathed. She pointed up at the side of the ditch and, even in the darkness and the gathering mist, Michael could see that there was someone standing there. Someone tall. Someone Michael was certain could only be Andrew Scutt.

'So zap him with the torch,' Michael whispered back.

'I can't,' Stephanie muttered. 'I can't reach it.' She pulled Jack closer to her and put her index finger to her lips as they all stayed still.

Andrew stood above them, looking around in the gloom. Michael figured he was probably listening for any sounds that would give one of his competitors away. Flat on his face in the ditch, Michael ached to get the torch and shine it on Andrew. At the same time he knew that if he moved too much in an attempt to reach the flashlight, the dry leaves around him would instantly alert the other boy, and he didn't want that. Instead, Michael could only try to get more comfortable, pushing out one hand to lift himself out of the dirt.

As he did so, his fingers closed on something soft and he wondered what it was. It only took him a second to realize that it was a cobweb. Even in the darkness, Michael could see the large spider emerge quickly from its lair in the ditch wall and scuttle hastily out on to the web he'd disturbed.

Michael hated spiders. He watched it nervously, his heart thudding so hard against his ribs that he feared Andrew would hear it.

Stephanie looked down and saw the spider too, but she merely pressed her finger against her lips again.

On the bank above them, Andrew still stood motionless, trying to hear or see figures moving through the black night and the silver mist.

Michael glanced at his companions. Jack was staring at the spider in fascination, while Stephanie was looking apprehensively from Michael's face to the spider and back again, clearly wondering whether Michael was going to give them away.

Michael definitely did not *want* to give away their position – especially not to Andrew Scutt of all people – but he knew that he was going to have to move soon. The spider was creeping slowly towards his outstretched fingers. Any moment now it would crawl on to his hand, and then Michael knew he would instinctively jump to get away from it.

At last, Andrew Scutt turned and walked away from the edge of the ditch. Michael breathed a sigh of relief, rolled away from the spider and picked up Stephanie's torch. Then he scrambled to his feet and leaned against the other side of the stream bed, trying to catch his breath, waiting for his heart to stop pounding.

'I thought he was going to see us,' Stephanie said quietly.

'So did I,' Michael agreed. 'But when I saw that spider, I thought I was going to have to move.'

'It was only a spider, Michael,' Jack said, grinning.

Michael laughed and reached forward to ruffle the lad's hair. 'You're a braver man than I am, Jack,' he said with a smile.

'Come on,' Stephanie whispered. 'We'd better keep moving down to the bottom of the hill.'

Michael nodded and was about to follow Stephanie when he glanced out over the top of the ditch and stopped in his tracks. 'Hang on a minute,' he said, looking around in the gloom. 'How long have we been playing?'

'About forty minutes,' Stephanie told him. 'Why?'

'We caught Jacob, right?' Michael said. 'And you saw Simone get caught as well.'

Stephanie nodded impatiently. 'Yeah, so what?'

Michael motioned for Stephanie to look out across the fields. She straightened up and peered out into the night.

'Well, if people have been found,' Michael said, 'why can't we see their torches? They'd still be standing where they were caught, wouldn't they? But I can't see anyone!'

'We haven't heard anything either,' Jack pointed out.

'That could be because of the wind,' Stephanie suggested. 'I mean, Andrew Scutt was standing right above us and he never heard us, did he?'

'The wind isn't as strong as it was when we started though, and we should still be able to see torches,' Michael protested. 'I think we should go back the way we came, see if the others are back there. Perhaps everyone else has been found and the game's been cancelled or something.'

'No. Everyone stays where they are until the last person's won,' Stephanie insisted. 'Those are the rules.'

'So where are they, then?' Michael demanded. 'And listen.'

All three of them stood still, listening intently for the slightest sound.

'The wind's dropped,' Michael insisted. 'And yet we *still* can't hear anyone else.'

'That's because everyone's trying to be quiet so they don't get caught,' Stephanie pointed out. 'And the mist's thicker now. It's harder to see anything.'

'Look, there,' Jack said, pointing into the night.

Michael saw it – a dull yellowish light that gleamed on the other side of the field. It glowed for a second, then it was gone.

'Someone else is still playing,' Stephanie insisted. 'They must be. And we know Andrew is because we've just seen him.'

'Well, let's go that way, then,' Michael said, gesturing with the torch. 'Perhaps we can catch someone . . .'

Stephanie hesitated for a moment, then she nodded. The three of them clambered cautiously up out of the ditch and set off across the dark field. Michael kept as low as he could and hoped the mist would hide him.

Now that the howling wind had dropped, the silence that had replaced it was quite unnerving. Michael found himself glancing left and right nervously as he walked, even though he could see very little in the impenetrable blackness.

The dull, yellow light flashed again, this time away to their left.

'Come on, let's head towards that light,' Michael suggested. 'At least we know someone must be over there.'

Stephanie, who was leading the way, nodded and turned, but as she did so, she tripped and almost fell.

Michael shone the torch briefly at the ground to see what had caused her to stumble. It was a pair of yellow wellington boots.

Stephanie reached for one and held it up. 'Can I have the torch for a moment?' she asked Michael, keeping her voice low.

He handed the torch over and Stephanie shone it inside the boot.

'I thought so. These are Simone's,' Stephanie said, reading a name tag inside the boot. 'But where is she?'

Michael shrugged and looked all around the field. There was nobody to be seen. 'Perhaps it's some kind of joke,' he suggested.

'What's this?' Jack wanted to know. He was kneeling on the ground pointing at a pile of white dust close to the wellington boots.

Michael knelt beside Jack and examined the dust, dipping one finger into the powdery substance. 'It's ash,' he said quietly, rubbing it between his fingers. 'Like something's been burned.'

'Simone got caught, so now she's trying to make out she's disappeared!' Stephanie said. 'I tell you what, I bet she's hiding around here somewhere.' And with that, Stephanie switched the torch on and swept the beam three hundred and sixty degrees around them. 'Come on, Simone,' she said, smiling. 'Show yourself!' But the torchlight revealed nothing except that the wispy, silvery mist was rapidly becoming a heavy, grey fog.

'What are you doing?' Michael snapped. 'Someone will see us!'

'That's what you want, isn't it?'

'No. I just want to know where everyone else is,' Michael explained, feeling slightly uneasy.

'You must be right. This must be some kind of joke,' Stephanie said. 'That's the only reason I can think of for why we can't see or hear anyone else. And it would explain Simone's boots. The others are probably just trying to scare us.'

'Or scare *me*, you mean,' Michael put in, his temper frayed by his anxiety. 'Is that the plan?

Frighten the city boy? How do I know you're not in on it too?'

Stephanie looked angrily at him. 'How could you say that?' she snapped.

'I'm sorry, I didn't mean it,' Michael apologized.

'You should know me better than that.'

'I said I didn't mean it,' Michael insisted. 'I think we're all getting a bit jumpy.'

'I'm not,' Jack beamed.

'Come on, let's keep walking,' Stephanie suggested, striding off through the thick grass.

Michael waited uncertainly for a moment, then realized that she had the torch and that he would be completely lost if he found himself alone in the fog. He set off after her. 'Where are we going?' he asked. 'Are you sure you still know where we are?'

'It's OK. Trust me,' Stephanie told him.

'But how do you know we're going the right way?' Michael demanded.

'I just do,' Stephanie sighed wearily.

'Well, are we heading back to my house,

or back to where we all started playing?' Michael enquired.

'Back to your house,' Stephanie replied. 'I'm bored with the game now.'

'But my house is *that* way,' Michael said, jabbing a finger off to his left.

'No it isn't,' Stephanie protested. 'I've lived here—'

'Oh, stop arguing,' Jack interrupted. 'We're lost, aren't we?'

All three of them stood still, the wind rising slightly and stirring the thick silver fog that surrounded them.

'Jack's right. We *are* lost, aren't we?' Michael echoed, looking at Stephanie.

Stephanie sighed. 'Well, I *think* your house is this way,' she said, and walked on through the tangled grass.

Michael sighed and followed, and Jack hopped along behind, seemingly the least concerned of the trio.

It seemed to be growing colder by the second and, despite the fact that Michael was wearing a thick coat, a sweatshirt and a T-shirt, he found that he was beginning to shiver. He forgot about that for a moment, though, when he stepped on something hard.

He dropped to his knees to retrieve the object. 'Stephanie,' he said quietly, holding what he'd found out in front of him. 'Look at this.'

Stephanie drew closer and peered at what Michael had in his hand. 'It's a torch,' she said, a note of puzzlement in her voice.

'It's Andrew Scutt's torch,' Michael told her. 'I remember it.' He flicked it on and off. 'And it's still working.'

'What are those?' Stephanie wanted to know, pointing at four indentations on one side of the torch's plastic grip. The marks made it look as if the torch had been squeezed in a powerful hand.

'It looks as if the plastic's melted,' Michael said,

peering at the marks. 'But what could have burned it like that?'

Stephanie shone the torch around, and something caught Michael's eye. On the ground, just where he'd picked up the torch, was more of the white ash they had found near Simone's wellington boots. Michael pointed to it.

Stephanie said nothing. She did, however, keep her own torch switched on.

'I thought you didn't want to lose the game,' Michael said.

Stephanie smiled grimly. 'I didn't, but I think you're right,' she confessed. 'Something weird's going on. Maybe it's just some stupid joke, but the game must have been called off. I think we should concentrate on getting back to your house now.'

Michael nodded and switched on Andrew's shiny red torch. The bright beam of torchlight cut reassuringly through the darkness, but fog still clouded the view ahead.

'Can I have a go with the torch?' Jack asked Michael hopefully.

Michael hesitated a moment, but then handed the flashlight to the smaller lad, watching as he ran back and forth, waving the torch around.

'It won't take us long now,' Stephanie said in a determined voice, and Michael wondered whether she was trying to reassure him and Jack, or herself.

They trekked onwards, their route taking them up a hill, through some trees and then down through another field. Michael's legs were aching and he found himself breathing heavily. That made him think of Jack.

'You'd have thought all this traipsing about would have made Jack's asthma worse,' he remarked to Stephanie. 'But I haven't heard him wheezing for a while.'

Stephanie stopped. 'You're right,' she agreed. 'He has gone very quiet. Are you all right, Jack?'

There was nothing but silence.

Stephanie turned a complete circle, shining her torch into the gloomy night. Michael followed the direction of the beam, but he could see nothing but grass and shadowy trees looming out of the fog.

Jack was gone.

'Jack!' Stephanie called, frantically.

'Jack!' echoed Michael, cursing the fog that obscured their vision.

Stephanie swept the torch back and forth across the night-soaked countryside, but its powerful beam revealed nothing but trees, bushes, tangled grasses and the ever-thickening fog.

Michael ran back up the slope they'd just descended. He could hear Stephanie following right behind him. 'He must have wandered off without our realizing,' Michael said, stopping and looking left and right for any sign of the lad.

'We've got to find him, Michael,' Stephanie said anxiously, her eyes filling with tears.

'Don't worry. We'll find him,' Michael assured

her. 'I promise you, we're not going anywhere until we have.'

Stephanie wiped her eyes, still shining the torch over the ground. 'Look! Over there,' she gasped.

The torchlight was shining on something plastic in the grass. Stephanie and Michael ran towards it. But as soon as she saw what it was, Stephanie burst into tears.

It was Jack's inhaler. But the plastic was melted and, as with Andrew Scutt's torch and Simone's wellington boots, there was a thick coating of silvery-grey ash all over the inhaler and on the ground around it.

'If he's lost this and he has an asthma attack, something awful could happen!' Stephanie sobbed in horror.

'It must have fallen out of his pocket when he was running,' Michael said firmly. 'Hang on to it and we'll give it back to him when we find him.'

'Michael, I'm serious. If Jack doesn't have his inhaler he could actually *die*!' Stephanie wailed.

Michael squinted through the night and saw a glimmer of yellow light about a hundred metres ahead. 'Over there,' he said, pointing towards the light.

'Jack!' Stephanie shouted, running towards the light.

Michael followed her.

'Stay where you are, Jack,' Stephanie panted.

'He must be using the torch to show us where he is,' Michael said.

'Nearly there, Jack,' yelled Stephanie.

They were less than fifty metres away when the light flickered and went out.

'Jack!' Stephanie screamed. 'Put the torch back on!'

Michael ran on, pulling ahead of Stephanie as if they were in some kind of bizarre race. 'I'll get him,' he called over his shoulder. 'Jack!' he shouted again, slowing down as he saw a wooden fence loom out of the fog in front of him.

He clambered up the fence, pausing as he

reached the top. To his delight, he heard heavy, rasping breathing a short distance away to his right. 'Jack,' he gasped, a huge sense of relief sweeping through him.

Michael swung himself over the fence and dropped down on the other side. But immediately his foot slipped and he felt himself tumbling, over and over. The hillside was steep and he was dizzy by the time he reached the bottom. Gasping for breath, he struggled to his feet and began to haul himself back up the hill.

By the time he reached the top his legs were throbbing with the effort of the climb, but he forced himself on. When he reached the wooden fence he realized he'd found the top of the hill once more. However, he could no longer hear Jack's breathing. And, as he looked around, another thought struck him: where was Stephanie?

He could see no torchlight and he couldn't hear her footsteps at all. First Simone, then Andrew, then Jack, now Stephanie! What was going on?

Michael felt himself start to panic and swallowed hard. Stephanie had probably followed him over the fence and slipped, just as he had done.

Suddenly, echoing through the darkness, came an eerie howl. It sounded exactly like a wolf and Michael shivered. Then he remembered the stray dog he had spotted earlier in the evening. *Not a wolf*, he told himself firmly. *This is England, not Transylvania! It's just the stray dog from earlier – or maybe a fox*.

The darkness, the fog and the strange events of the night were making his imagination work overtime, Michael realized. He leaned against the fence and forced himself to calm down. Gradually, his pounding heart slowed and his breathing grew steady again.

And as it did so, Michael noticed that he could feel a soft, woollen fabric beneath his fingers. He frowned and peered at it in the darkness. It was Stephanie's coat. It was caught on the fence, just hanging there, as if Stephanie had simply slipped out of it and left it behind.

'Stephanie!' Michael called, frantically.

There was no response. But then, once again, he heard that low, wheezy breathing that he'd heard earlier. 'Jack!' Michael yelled. 'Stephanie! One of you answer me!' His voice seemed to echo in the night as if it was bouncing off the fog around him.

The low rasping sound was now louder, closer to him. He spun round and smiled, for there was a light less than twenty metres away. But the smile died on his lips as he realized that it wasn't torchlight. This light was flickery and golden, like candlelight.

Now it was moving towards him, suspended at eye level. It drew closer still, getting brighter until the glare was so great that Michael had to shield his face, and, all the time, the wheezing, rasping breathing grew louder. It reminded him of a growling dog.

'Is that you, Jack?' Michael whispered, his voice quavering.

The ball of light was only a few metres away now

and Michael could see it clearly at last. It was the glow of a lantern. The flickering flame cast a pool of dull light. And now, besides the rasping breaths, Michael became aware of something much worse: a terrible smell that caught in his nostrils and throat. The smell of burnt meat.

Michael tried to back away, but the wooden fence behind him blocked his way. Fear held his gaze glued to the light. And then the lantern was raised close to a face and, at last, Michael could see who was carrying it.

With the stink in his nostrils and the sound of that heavy breathing in his ears, he opened his mouth to scream, but no sound came out and all he could do was stare in horrified disbelief.

In front of him stood a man, or at least what had once been a man. Charred, blackened skin was peeling from his face and hands like old paint. Long strips of it hung like burnt apple peel from his jaw bone and forehead, and all at once, Michael knew that he was looking at the dead Farmer Axby.

Farmer Axby opened his mouth, his burned lips parting to reveal a bloated, swollen tongue. 'I can see you, Michael Lewis,' he rasped.

And in that split second, Michael realized why there had been only ashes where the other players should have been.

'I can see you,' the hideous farmer said again, and this time there was an unmistakable note of triumph in his voice. With one stinking breath, Farmer Axby blew out the lantern.

And there was only darkness.

TRUE COLOURS

The words buzzed like angry bees in her ears. Carrie Peterson leaned forward in the passenger seat of the car and eased the volume of the CD player up a notch, trying to drive the words away.

Her mother hadn't stopped talking since they'd left the house that morning. Or, at least, that's how it felt to Carrie. Not that this morning was any different to all the others. Every day it was the same earache.

'You did do your homework, didn't you, Carrie?' Mrs Peterson asked.

'Yes, Mum,' Carrie said, trying to concentrate on the music and zone her mum out as much as possible.

'And you did sign up for drama class after school, didn't you?' her mother continued.

'Yes, Mum,' answered Carrie, somehow keeping her fixed smile in place.

'Did you comb your hair this morning?' Mrs Peterson asked doubtfully, glancing at her.

'Yes, Mum.'

'It doesn't look like it.'

'It's supposed to look like this, Mum,' Carrie said, pulling down the sun visor on her side of the car. She inspected her image in the mirror, stroking a hand through her hair. Her natural colour was strawberry blonde but she'd recently added some pink highlights.

'I hope that dye washes out,' Mrs Peterson said, smoothing her own immaculately cut and styled blonde hair.

'It'll wash out after three days, Mum,' Carrie explained patiently. 'Just like the last one.'

'You mean the sky-blue one? The one your head of year threatened to give you a week's detention for?' Mrs Peterson enquired.

Carrie nodded. 'Mrs Rigby hasn't got a clue about how to dress. I wouldn't expect her to appreciate my hair or my fashion sense. Why is everyone so bothered about the way I look, anyway?' she went on, feeling mutinous. 'It's no one's business except mine. Just because most people don't get it, doesn't mean there's anything wrong with it. It's my style – just like yours is all designer labels.'

'At least my clothes are tidy. I'd look a bit ridiculous turning up for work dressed the way you are, wouldn't I?' Mrs Peterson pointed out.

Carrie glanced down at the outfit she'd so thoughtfully assembled for herself that day. Her bright green long-sleeved T-shirt, complete with a grinning face on the front, was worn under a red cardigan that had badges of various sizes pinned to either side of it. Her flared jeans were faded and threadbare on both knees, and her stripy socks were visible above her trainers. 'Didn't you ever experiment with fashion when you were my age?' Carrie asked with a sigh.

'Of course I did,' her mother replied. 'But that didn't include dyeing my hair so that it looked as if someone had put candy floss on my head!'

'Well, my real friends think that my style is cool and I like it. That's all that matters,' Carrie said firmly.

Her mum sighed and brought the car to a halt just past the school gates. Carrie reached into the back seat and dragged her latest pride and joy on to her lap. It was a large, customized, retro canvas bag.

'Have you got your PE kit?' her mother asked, as Carrie clambered out of the car.

Carrie smiled and dangled the bag before her mum's gaze.

'I doubt any of the other girls have a bag like that,' Mrs Peterson remarked.

'That's the whole point, Mum,' Carrie sighed. She slammed the car door behind her and heard the electric window whir as it was lowered.

'Have a good day,' her mum called. 'Try not to annoy too many people.' She gave Carrie a wink to let her know she was half joking.

'I'll do my best, Mum.' Carrie forced herself to smile. 'Are you working late again this evening?'

'It's difficult to say,' her mother replied. 'I'll do my best to be home by six, but you know it's not easy. See you later.'

Carrie nodded, watching as her mum drove away. 'No, Mum,' she murmured wearily. 'It's never easy, is it?'

'Well, I think it's great,' said Tess Walker. 'I wish I had a bag like it.'

Carrie smiled as she watched her friend Tess run an approving eye over the retro bag. It was lunch break and the first proper chance the girls had had to catch up. Carrie stepped nimbly out of the way as a younger boy ran past, quickly followed by a bunch of mates.

'Did you do all those designs yourself?' Tess asked, turning the bag back and forth.

Carrie nodded. 'And I sewed the patches on,' she said. 'My mum hates it, obviously. But she hates everything about my style.'

'All parents hate what we wear, do, say and listen to,' Tess grinned. 'It's their job.'

The two girls laughed, but they were abruptly interrupted by another voice.

'Which charity shop did you get the bag from, Carrie?'

Carrie rolled her eyes and turned in the direction of the voice.

'Or was it a jumble sale?' Lisa Jameson continued, smiling brightly. Behind her, the five girls who always followed Lisa around giggled nastily.

'Or maybe you just picked it up from the

local rubbish tip?' Lisa went on. There was more laughter.

'What's wrong, can't you afford a new bag?' Lisa demanded. 'Your mum earns enough money. She must be embarrassed, letting you come to school with something like that.' Lisa peered disdainfully at the bag. 'You should get her to buy you something decent.'

'I like this bag, thanks,' Carrie responded. 'Everyone has their own personal taste, you know.'

'Yes, I know, and yours is *terrible*,' Lisa replied. The girls around her laughed.

'Well, I'm not going to argue with you, Lisa,' Carrie said wearily, raising her voice so she could be heard over the chorus of laughter. She turned to walk away. 'Come on, Tess.'

'Go on, then,' Lisa called. 'Run away. Perhaps you'll find a nice fleece or a pair of trousers in the school dustbins.'

Carrie felt her cheeks burn as she and Tess walked off, the other girls' laughter ringing in her ears.

'I hate her,' Tess said as they made their way from the playground towards the girls' toilets.

Carrie didn't speak. For a moment she thought she was going to cry but that feeling quickly gave way to one of anger. They walked into the toilets and Carrie crossed to one of the sinks and studied her reflection in the mirror. She spun one of the taps and began washing her hands.

'Lisa's frightened of being different,' Carrie said angrily. 'She wants to be like everyone else. She wants to look like them, talk like them and act like them, and those girls that hang around with her are just like sheep. They're all pathetic.'

Tess nodded in agreement.

'First Mum and now Lisa Jameson,' groaned Carrie, drying her hands. 'Perhaps my mum switched babies when I was born. She likes designer stuff and so does Lisa. My mum's got blonde hair and so has Lisa.'

'So have you, *naturally*,' Tess pointed out. 'It's just that you dye yours a different colour every month.'

'Well, you know what they say: variety is the spice of life! Next month I think I'll go for bright red,' Carrie laughed. 'Or maybe luminous green. That'll really get everyone going.'

Both girls chuckled, the sound filling the bathroom. Carrie looked at her reflection in the mirror once more and felt her mood lift. It would take more than Lisa Jameson and her idiotic followers to worry her. She ran a hand through her hair and grinned at her mirror image.

When the bell sounded for the end of the school day, Carrie trooped outside with her fellow pupils, who scattered in different directions as they headed home. Carrie soon found herself alone at the school gates. As she paused to heave her bag on to her shoulder, someone stepped out in front of her. Carrie felt her heart sink.

'Like the cardigan, Carrie,' giggled Lisa Jameson. '*Not*.'

The girls around Lisa laughed as they gazed at

Carrie's red cardigan with its carefully placed badges.

Carrie opened her mouth to say something, then decided against it, so she stepped around Lisa and began walking home.

'It's the same colour as my dog's blanket!' one of the girls called after her.

'Perhaps it *is* your dog's blanket,' one of the others added to more laughter. 'It looks like it.'

Just ignore them, Carrie told herself. *They're not worth your time*.

Carrie kept walking but the others were following and they wouldn't shut up.

Lisa stepped up to Carrie, a look of triumph on her face. 'You're just too emotional, Carrie,' she smirked. 'That's your trouble.'

Carrie stood still on the pavement as Lisa and the other girls ran off along the road, one of them turning to wave mockingly at Carrie.

'Idiots,' Carrie said under her breath, reaching for her mobile as she felt it vibrate. She pulled it from her jacket pocket, and saw that she had a text message. It was from her mum.

'Running late, can't pick you up. Could you and Mark do the dinner? Love, Mum.' Carrie sighed and dropped the mobile back into her pocket. 'Thanks, Mum,' she murmured. *This is turning into a really bad day*, she thought to herself, her earlier good mood forgotten.

'Hey, Carrie!'

'Amy.' Carrie beamed to see her cousin running towards her. 'What are you doing here?'

'I thought I'd check out the market in the park on my way home from school,' Amy replied.

Carrie's smile broadened. 'I'll join you.' She and Amy had been friends all their lives, even though they now went to different schools. The girls walked through the iron gates of the park.

'How come you're not getting a lift home tonight?' Amy asked.

'Mum's working late again,' Carrie sighed. 'Mark

and I have to get dinner ready for when Dad gets home.'

'I saw a fire engine this morning and your dad was driving,' Amy said. 'He waved to me as he went past.'

'I hope he wasn't called to a big fire,' Carrie said anxiously. 'I always worry about him when he's working.'

The two girls walked on in silence for a moment. Then the market came into view. It was a symphony of colours, smells, sights and sounds. The coloured awnings seemed to create a rainbow effect as Carrie looked at them. And the smell of frying bacon, onions and coffee coming from one stall made her feel hungry.

The girls reached the first of the stalls and stopped to look at the handmade jewellery that had been carefully laid out on a black velvet cloth.

Amy picked up a silver daisy brooch with a tiger's eye at its centre, and held it against Carrie's cardigan. 'It looks good on you,' she said.

Carrie smiled, but shook her head when she saw the price. 'Yeah, but I can't afford twenty quid,' she replied.

Amy replaced the brooch and the two girls moved on, past more stalls selling everything from hand-drawn charcoal sketches to scented candles.

'Let's have a look over there,' Carrie said, nodding towards a stall displaying a range of books and magazines. 'I need something new to read.'

Most of the hardbacks on display were discoloured with age and many no longer had their dust jackets. Amy inspected the spines to check the titles, while Carrie picked up a book and leafed through the yellowed pages.

'Look at the cover of this one!' Amy exclaimed, pointing out a book about astronomy. It showed a silver-painted telescope surrounded by fading stars that made up the name of the book's author.

Carrie smiled but she was more interested in the old magazines that were laid out at one end of the stall. 'Some of these magazines are over thirty years old,' she said, picking up a copy of *Film Review*. 'They're practically antiques!'

'All of them ten pence, sweetheart,' said the old lady who ran the stall. 'Take your time deciding.'

She smiled thinly at Carrie, pulling her coat more tightly around herself. Her hair was long and grey, held in a ponytail by a wide, black velvet band. She had thin, pinched features and the bluest eyes Carrie had ever seen.

'Are you going to buy anything?' Amy asked.

Carrie didn't answer. She wasn't looking at the magazines, but at the right arm of the old woman running the stall. She had her hand shoved firmly into the money belt she wore around her waist and, Carrie noted, she never removed it, not even to serve her customers.

'What are you getting, Carrie?' Amy persisted.

Carrie tore her gaze away from the old woman and scanned the covers of the magazines. One of them suddenly caught her eye. 'Look at this,' she said, picking it up. 'I've got to get this. Look at the date on it. It's the same as my birthday.'

'It comes with a free gift too,' Amy noticed. 'Look – stuck to the cover.'

'Can I take this one, please?' Carrie asked the old lady, handing the magazine over and digging in her purse for a ten-pence piece.

'Good choice, dear,' the old lady said, putting the magazine down and extending her left hand to take the money. 'It's very rare. It'll be worth much more than ten pence in a few years.' She reached out to hand the magazine back to Carrie, but before doing so, the old lady deftly twisted the free gift away from the cover and dropped it into her coat pocket.

'Doesn't that come with the magazine?' Carrie asked, a little irritated at being denied her free gift.

The old lady merely shook her head.

'It was a mood ring, wasn't it?' Carrie pressed, pointing at the cover. 'Look, it says here on the cover that there's a chart inside to tell you what the different colours mean when the ring changes. I've always wanted a mood ring.'

'You wouldn't want that one, dear,' the old lady said firmly.

'Can I have the ring that goes with the magazine, please?' Carrie persisted.

'The *magazine* was ten pence, dear,' the old lady said coldly, glaring at Carrie with her icy blue eyes. 'Not the ring.' And, with that, she turned her back on Carrie and began tidying the books and magazines from her stall into the cardboard boxes beneath.

'How much do you want for the ring?' Carrie demanded, feeling exasperated. 'I really would like it.'

'I don't mean to be rude,' the woman said over her shoulder, 'but I've a lot to do, packing up my stall. If you're desperate for a ring, visit Bob's stall on the other side of the market. Lovely stuff, he has.'

As the woman hastily shoved magazines into cardboard boxes, Carrie could see that her face was flushed. It was clear that the old woman wanted her to go, but a streak of stubbornness kept Carrie rooted to the spot. She'd had a bad enough day, without people trying to swindle her. 'I'll give you fifty pence for it,' Carrie told the woman finally.

'The ring's not for sale, dear. It was the magazine I was selling, not the ring.'

Carrie and Amy looked quizzically at each other for a moment, then back at the old woman, who had managed to clear her stall with amazing speed. The remaining books and magazines had been put away, and she had piled the boxes into a rusty shopping trolley. The girls watched as the old lady hurried off, pushing the trolley in front of her.

'It was only a cheap old mood ring, Carrie,' Amy said. 'Come on, let's see what else we can find before the other stalls pack up.'

Carrie nodded and the two girls moved on through the market. They stopped at a stall selling hats and tried a few on. They bought chocolate chip cookies from a cake stall and ate them hungrily. Then, just as Carrie was thinking about heading home, Amy spotted a Celtic-style cross that she couldn't resist. She bought it and hung it around her neck.

'It looks great,' Carrie told her, admiring it. 'Do you want to get anything else?'

'No, thanks,' Amy replied. 'It's getting cold now. I think I'd better go home.'

'Good idea,' Carrie agreed, and the girls turned towards the gates.

As they were leaving, something shiny caught Carrie's eye. A small metal object was lying in the grass, close to the old woman's now empty magazine stall.

Carrie hurried across and bent down to retrieve the item. 'It's the mood ring!' she exclaimed in surprise. 'It must have fallen out of the old lady's pocket when she was packing her stuff away.'

'Are you going to keep it?' Amy asked.

'Well, I bought the magazine it was stuck to, didn't I?' Carrie pointed out.

Amy nodded. 'Yeah, and it was supposed to be a free gift.'

Carrie looked at the ring thoughtfully for a moment, then dropped it into her pocket.

'That lady probably hasn't even realized she's lost it,' Amy said. 'And now I really must get home. My mum will be wondering where I am.'

'Me too,' Carrie agreed. 'I can't leave Mark to get the dinner on his own, he'll kill me.'

Amy laughed and waved and the girls hurried off in opposite directions.

Carrie grinned to herself. For the first time that day she felt really happy.

The house was warm when Carrie got home and the delicious aroma of cooking wafted through from the kitchen.

'It's me!' she called, kicking off her shoes.

'About time,' her brother answered from the kitchen. 'I've already started the dinner.'

Carrie felt in her pocket for the mood ring. Her

fingers closed around it and she withdrew it eagerly, turning it over and over in the palm of her hand. It glistened darkly in the light. Slowly, she pushed it on to her right index finger.

It was a perfect fit. Carrie smiled – something about it just felt right. It was almost as if it had been made for her. She looked down at the magazine cover. 'LOOK INSIDE TO SEE HOW TO USE YOUR MOOD RING', it said.

'I'll come and help in a minute, Mark,' Carrie called distractedly, heading for the living-room.

'Dad rang and said he'll be home in about half an hour,' her brother shouted back.

Carrie nodded and sat down on the sofa, flicking through the old magazine. 'DOES THE RING MATCH YOUR MOOD?' proclaimed the lettering across the centre pages. Carrie scanned the colour chart:

LIGHT BLUE – Happy

PINK – Optimistic

DARK BLUE – Sad

RED – Angry

PURPLE – Afraid

BROWN – Confused

GREEN – Jealous

ORANGE – Content

YELLOW – Ill

GREY – Tired

Curiously, Carrie checked the colour of the ring against the colour chart before her. The stone was light blue. She nodded. 'Not just a perfect fit, then,' she said to herself happily. 'It's got my mood right, too.'

'Carrie, are you going to come and help me or what?' her brother yelled from the kitchen.

She glanced at the ring, wondering if it had changed colour. No. Apparently there wasn't a colour for 'irritated by older brother'. She smiled to herself. 'I'm coming,' she shouted.

Carrie had just got to her feet when the phone rang. 'I'll get it,' Carrie called, reaching for the receiver. 'It's probably Mum to say she's on her way.'

She picked up the phone. 'Hello?' she said.

'Hello, is that Carrie?' said a slightly nasal voice at the other end of the line.

'Yes,' Carrie replied.

'It's Caroline,' said the caller. Caroline was her mum's personal assistant. 'Your mum asked me to remind you to switch off the cooker after you've finished making dinner.'

'OK, thanks, Caroline,' Carrie said wearily. 'Did she say what time she'd be home?'

'No, sorry. She's in a meeting at the moment.'

'So you don't know how long she's going to be?' Carrie asked.

'No, but it could be an hour or more. You know what these meetings are like.'

'Yes, I know,' Carrie said, unhappily. 'OK. Thanks for calling, Caroline. Bye.' She put the receiver down and sighed heavily.

As she took her hand away from the phone she glanced at the mood ring. The stone was still light blue but even as she watched, it began to darken.

Like day becoming night, the shade of blue changed until it was deep navy. Carrie didn't have to check the colour chart to know what navy meant. It was the colour of sadness. The ring seemed to be working perfectly.

Carrie headed for the kitchen.

'You took your time,' said her brother as she walked in. 'Who was that on the phone?'

'Caroline,' Carrie told him. 'But she didn't know what time Mum would be home.'

'Great,' Mark sighed.

As he spoke, Carrie glanced around the kitchen. It looked as if a bomb had gone off. There were empty food cartons on the worktops, potato peelings on the floor by the sink, and although the kitchen table hadn't been laid, milk had been spilt on it.

'Mark, anyone would think you were six, not sixteen!' Carrie snapped. 'Look at the mess you've made!'

'I've been getting the dinner ready,' her brother

explained, pointing to the casserole bubbling in the oven. 'If you'd been here to help, you could have tidied up.'

'Why should I tidy up your mess?' Carrie demanded.

'OK, OK, take it easy. Mess doesn't usually bother you; I've seen your bedroom,' Mark laughed.

'Oh, ha ha! Well, *you* made this mess so *you* tidy it up – otherwise Dad won't be very happy when he comes in,' Carrie replied, feeling unreasonably annoyed by Mark's attempt at humour.

'At least give me a hand.'

'Forget it!'

'Thanks,' Mark sighed irritably. 'You weren't here to help cook, you could at least help with the clearing up.'

'Don't tell me what to do!' Carrie yelled, completely losing her temper. 'I'm sick of you trying to boss me around just because you're older.'

Mark didn't say anything. Carrie could see him eyeing her warily. It was very annoying.

'And don't look at me like that,' she went on. 'Just because I won't clear up your mess doesn't mean there's anything wrong with me. You're just selfish and I'm not putting up with it any more!' Carrie suddenly realized that she was trembling all over.

'All right, all right,' Mark said soothingly, sounding genuinely worried. 'I'm sorry I made such a mess. It's never upset you like this before.'

Realizing that was true, Carrie raised her hands in a gesture of surrender. As she did, she noticed that the mood ring was now glowing bright red: the colour of anger. She glared at her brother but kept her mouth tightly closed for fear of what she might say next. She still felt angry, but she also had a strong feeling that she might have been a little unfair. She took some deep breaths, and felt the anger slowly start to subside.

'I'll help you tidy up,' Carrie said quietly, once she could trust herself to speak.

Mark nodded, watching her closely, clearly

uncertain how she was going to react next. Then he started to tidy up the kitchen.

Carrie stood motionless for a moment, unable to believe she had lost her temper with Mark like that. He was right, it wasn't like her. She tried to tell herself that it was just because she'd had a bad day, but something at the back of her mind told her that wasn't entirely true.

She shook her head in puzzlement and began to help her brother. As she reached out to pick up a carton of gravy mix, she saw that the mood ring had changed colour again. The angry red was now replaced by the brown of confusion.

Carrie nodded, agreeing with the ring. Then she heard the front door open.

'It's only me,' called a tired voice.

Their dad wandered into the kitchen and sat down wearily on one of the chairs. He looked shattered. His eyes were red rimmed and Carrie could see the dirt on his cheeks and hands.

'Are you all right, Dad?' she asked.

He shook his head. 'There was a fire at a warehouse just outside town,' he said grimly. 'I've been there for hours. It took us all day to get it under control. Part of the roof collapsed and two people were killed; we just couldn't get them out in time.'

Carrie and her brother drew close to their dad, seeing the exhaustion and distress on his face and wanting to be supportive.

'I think I'll go up to bed if you don't mind,' he said, smiling at them. 'I'm afraid I won't be very good company tonight and I'm worn out. Sorry about the dinner.'

Mark shook his head. 'It's nothing, don't worry,' he said. He and Carrie exchanged a glance and Carrie felt a stab of guilt. Whatever had made her lose her temper paled into insignificance beside her dad's story.

Carrie gave her dad a hug before he went upstairs. She felt dreadful thinking about the people who had died, and sorry for the terrible day her dad had faced, but she also felt a twinge of resentment. *Another great family night in*, she thought to herself. 'I think I'll go to bed too,' she told her brother.

'Great,' Mark groaned. 'Shall I eat dinner on my own, then?'

Carrie could only shrug as she turned and headed for the stairs. As she put her hand on the banister she saw that the mood ring was now a dull grey. 'Tired,' Carrie said aloud, noticing the colour. 'Accurate, aren't you?'

The rain had been falling steadily ever since Carrie woke up that morning. Now, during her lunch break, she sat in the common room watching the raindrops course down the glass of the school windows. 'I hate the rain,' she murmured to herself.

Her eyelids felt heavy with tiredness. Her sleep the previous night had been constantly interrupted by bad dreams. She shivered as she remembered one in which she had imagined a large, dark figure standing over her, pressing a pillow down on to her face until she couldn't breathe.

Carrie rubbed her eyes. Because of the rain, no one had been allowed outside at lunch-time. She looked away from the window and glanced around the room. There was a constant background babble of conversation as the other kids laughed and chatted.

Some magazines on a nearby table caught Carrie's eye, so she reached for one to flick through. As she did, she saw Lisa Jameson striding towards her, her usual little clique in tow.

'Nice ring. Which pound shop did you get it from, Carrie?' Lisa sneered, and the other girls burst out laughing.

Carrie tried to ignore them. She gazed fixedly at the magazine.

'Which designer is it made by?' Lisa continued loudly. 'Oxfam or the Salvation Army?'

That provoked a second round of giggling.

'You'd better be careful that cheap metal doesn't

turn your finger green,' Lisa went on, revelling in the fact that she had an audience. 'I bet your mum doesn't like it. Too cheap for her, isn't it? Mind you, I think you're a bit too cheap for your mum altogether. That's probably why she never spends any time with you.'

Carrie felt anger building up inside her, but she realized that it was tinged with something else. A feeling much stronger than rage. She stole a glance at her mood ring, expecting to see it glowing red to reflect her fury. She was a little surprised to see that it was bright green: the colour of jealousy. *Why am I jealous of Lisa?* Carrie wondered.

'Mind you, no one spends much time with you, do they?' Lisa murmured, wandering idly away from Carrie towards the other side of the room.

Carrie felt her patience snap. She shot to her feet in fury and took a couple of steps towards Lisa before she knew what she was doing. Lisa smiled and Carrie realized that the other girl was pleased to have got a reaction from her. That thought made her stop.

'Perhaps if you had some idea of how to fit in, instead of trying to pretend you're such an individual, you'd have some friends,' Lisa continued, clearly trying to provoke Carrie further. 'You wouldn't have to be jealous of people like me then, would you?'

Is that why I'm jealous? Carrie wondered. *Do I really want friends like Lisa's?* She frowned and glanced down at the mood ring. It was still green for jealousy, glinting in the light like a cat's eye. Even though the ring appeared to confirm Lisa's snide remark, Carrie couldn't bear to think that Lisa was right.

'Perhaps you should look at the things I wear, Carrie,' Lisa was saying airily. 'You might pick up some tips.'

Carrie felt rage burn through her again. This time she whirled around and headed for the door. She wanted to be as far away from Lisa Jameson's prying eyes and bitchy comments as possible. As she walked out of the room, she heard Lisa and her friends laughing again. The mood ring still shone green.

Carrie picked up the TV remote and jabbed one of the buttons.

'Is this what our evening's going to consist of?' her dad chuckled. 'Four hours of soap operas and reality TV?'

'No, Dad,' Carrie told him, pushing a piece of pizza into her mouth. 'It's only *three* hours.'

They both laughed and continued eating their takeaway. Carrie felt happier than she had in ages. Her dad had been off duty all day and just seeing him when she'd arrived home from school had lifted her spirits. When he'd told her that he had the rest of the night off and that they could order in a pizza, she hadn't needed to look at the mood ring to see its colour; she knew it would be showing light blue – for happiness.

'Did Mum say what time she was coming home?' Carrie asked.

'No. She's having dinner with some people from her company tonight so it'll probably be late.'

'And Mark's at his friend's house, so that means we don't have to save *him* any pizza,' Carrie added.

Her dad laughed and grabbed another slice. 'I'd better get some of this for myself before you scoff the lot,' he teased. 'I don't know where you put it all. You must have hollow legs.'

Carrie reached for another piece of pizza, but stopped suddenly when she felt her stomach ache as if it had been punched by a cold and invisible fist. She sat back in her chair, hoping that the feeling would subside.

'Are you OK, Carrie?' her dad asked, looking worried.

She nodded. 'I just feel cold suddenly,' she said, gazing blankly at the TV screen as she tried to work out what was wrong. She could feel the hairs on the back of her neck standing up, and the chill that had struck her stomach was now seeping through her whole body. Carrie swallowed hard, not understanding why she felt so uncomfortable. And so *frightened*.

Her dad was still looking at her with concern when his mobile rang. He hesitated a moment then picked it up. 'Hello,' he said. Carrie watched his face. 'When?' he asked. 'Whereabouts?'

Carrie saw his expression darken.

'How many are involved?' he demanded, listening intently. Then he nodded. 'All right. Give me five minutes.' He closed the phone and got to his feet. 'Are you going to be all right, Carrie? I'm afraid I've got to go,' he said, already heading for the door. 'There's a house fire on the other side of town. It's badly out of control and spreading.'

'It's OK, Dad, I'll be fine,' Carrie said, a little sadly.

'At least now you get to finish all the pizza,' he told her with a grin.

Carrie followed him to the front door and

watched as he pulled on his coat and shoes and sprinted out to his car.

'Be careful, Dad,' she called as he reversed out into the road, spun the wheel and sped away. She watched the car's tail-lights disappear around the corner then closed the front door and headed back to the living-room. She couldn't resist a glance at her mood ring. It was purple: the colour of fear.

Carrie wasn't surprised; she got scared every time her dad was called to a big fire. The thought of him battling against the flames always made her nervous, but, for some unknown reason, this time she felt even more uneasy than usual. Perhaps because she'd felt a surge of fear even before the phone rang. It was almost as if she had somehow known that bad news was coming. But Carrie knew that was crazy. It had been a coincidence, nothing more. Hadn't it?

Again she gazed at the ring, and saw that it had changed colour once more. It was now the muddy brown of confusion. Carrie smiled and shook her head, puzzled by how accurately the ring seemed to reflect her feelings. She looked at the remains of the pizza on the table, but she didn't feel like eating any more. It was too early to go to bed, so she curled up on the sofa to watch TV.

The evening seemed to pass terribly slowly, but Carrie was determined to wait up until her dad got home. She had a cold feeling in the pit of her stomach. Something felt wrong. Something she couldn't put her finger on. A growing feeling of dread. Carrie knew she wouldn't be able to settle until her dad was back safe and sound, but the TV wasn't serving to distract her from the worries tumbling through her mind. She reached for a magazine and flicked through that instead, but the contents didn't register. Finally, she decided to see if some homework would occupy her thoughts. She fetched one of the reference books from her schoolbag, but the chapter she was supposed to read just didn't seem to make any sense. After reading one page twice Carrie decided to give up and make herself a cup of tea.

She was barely off the sofa when the phone rang. She snatched it up. 'Hello,' she said, nervously.

'Carrie, it's Dad,' said the voice at the other end of the line.

Immediately, Carrie felt a wave of relief sweep through her. 'I was worried about you, Dad,' she told him, balancing the receiver in the crook of her neck so that she could hold her right hand up in front of her face. The mood ring shone with the bright, light blue of happiness.

'I'm fine, sweetheart,' he told her. 'Listen to me, Carrie, that fire I was called to, it was at the Jameson family's house. You go to school with their daughter, don't you?'

'Lisa, yes. Why?' Carrie replied.

There was a moment's silence at the other end of the line, then her dad started speaking again. He sounded grim. 'The fire was out of control by the time the first fire engines arrived,' he said. 'They think a gas explosion started it, which is why it was so fierce. It ripped right through the house from the kitchen. The blast took out the whole first floor of the building like a bomb.'

Carrie sat down as she listened, her heart beating hard against her ribs.

'Both of Lisa's parents are in hospital now,' her dad went on. 'They were downstairs when it happened. They were lucky. But we couldn't save anyone who was upstairs . . .'

Carrie felt slightly sick as her father continued.

'I'm sorry, sweetheart,' he said softly, 'but I have to tell you because I know you're going to find out from someone and I think it's better you find out from me.'

'What is it, Dad?' Carrie asked quietly, although she thought she already knew what he was going to say next.

'Lisa Jameson's dead.'

The assembly hall at school was full the following

morning. As Carrie trooped slowly in with the rest of her class, the subdued atmosphere told her that news of Lisa Jameson's death had spread rapidly among everyone there. On the stage at the far end of the hall two teachers were speaking quietly, one of them dabbing at her eyes with a handkerchief. Even the youngest pupils, sitting right at the front of the hall, were silent.

Carrie sat down next to Tess.

'It's terrible about Lisa Jameson, isn't it?' Tess said.

Carrie nodded. 'I couldn't sleep last night,' she said. 'I know Lisa and I didn't get on but I would never have wished something like that on her.' She rubbed her face with both hands then gazed at the stage as the headmistress stood up to speak.

'As you probably all know by now,' Mrs Collet began in her most sombre tone, 'there was a terrible tragedy last night involving one of this school's pupils, Lisa Jameson, and her family.'

Carrie heard some sniffing from her left-hand

side and saw that Danielle Harrison, one of Lisa's friends, was crying softly.

'Lisa was a very popular girl,' Mrs Collet continued. 'Thoughtful, caring, hardworking and always ready to help others.'

Carrie shook her head slightly at that. *Thoughtful and caring?* Not the Lisa she'd known.

'She was a credit to the school and to her family and I know that you will all miss her,' Mrs Collet went on. 'So, I would like you all to stand now, and as a mark of respect for the Jameson family we shall observe a one-minute silence in memory of Lisa.'

The entire school rose as one.

Mrs Collet waited until everyone was on their feet then nodded. 'One minute's silence, starting now,' she said.

Carrie linked her hands in front of her but, as she did, she noticed that the mood ring had turned light blue. She blinked in disbelief and peered down at it again. It was definitely light blue – indicating *happiness*! Carrie frowned. She didn't feel happy about what had happened to Lisa. They might not have been friends, but she hadn't wished Lisa dead.

The hall remained silent, except that Carrie could now hear the muffled sounds of several people crying. At the same time, she felt the corners of her mouth lift in the beginnings of a smile. In horror, she realized that a broad, happy grin was spreading uncontrollably across her face. Carrie bowed her head, anxious that no one should see her, but the smile was growing.

Carrie couldn't understand what was happening to her. She bit the inside of her lip hard in an effort to stop the smile, but then, to her horror, she felt laughter bubbling up inside her, threatening to erupt in a peal of giggles.

Tess glanced sideways at her, clearly wondering what was wrong, but Carrie could only meet her puzzled stare with a grin.

And then it happened: Carrie burst out laughing. The sound exploded from her, sounding horribly loud in the silence of the hall. Tess nudged her hard in the ribs. Others turned to stare at her – some in surprise, some in anger or confusion. And Carrie tried desperately to stifle her laughter, but she couldn't.

'Shut up!' someone nearby hissed.

But Carrie was finding it impossible to stop laughing. She put a hand to her mouth to try and stifle the sound, but it was useless. She was laughing so hard that her belly was beginning to ache.

Out of the corner of her eye, she saw one of her teachers, Mr Wainwright, heading angrily in her direction. Yet still Carrie couldn't stop herself. The great bellows of laughter continued to shake her, the sound reverberating round the hall.

Carrie felt a hand on her arm, and still laughing like a maniac, she was dragged out of line by Mr Wainwright, who whispered something angrily in her ear about a lack of respect.

Heads turned in her direction as Carrie was

virtually pushed from the hall through the double doors that led out on to the playing-field.

'I've never seen behaviour like it,' snapped Mr Wainwright, as soon as they were outside. 'You should be ashamed of yourself!'

The blast of cold air that hit Carrie once she was outside acted like a bucket of cold water poured over her head, and Carrie finally managed to get the horrible laughter under control. She stood still, taking deep breaths.

Carrie could see that many of her fellow pupils were still gazing out at her through the hall windows, looking shocked and annoyed by her outburst. Danielle Harrison was crying and pointing at her angrily and as Carrie raised a hand to brush some hair away from her face, she noticed that the mood ring was now changing colour rapidly from the light blue of happiness to the purple of fear. At the same time, she found herself wondering whether Danielle and the rest of Lisa Jameson's offended friends might come after her. Her head spun.

'What do you think you were doing?' Mr Wainwright asked, furiously.

'I'm sorry. I just couldn't help it, sir,' Carrie tried to explain.

'Lisa Jameson died last night and all you can do is laugh,' the teacher barked. 'I'm surprised at you, Carrie. I thought you would have known better.'

'Sir, I couldn't help it,' Carrie insisted.

'You'll do a week's detention for that dreadful exhibition of disrespect, do you understand?' he hissed. 'Go to the detention room immediately. I don't think any of your teachers will want to see you today after that outburst. Your work will be brought in to you. Go on, go now.'

Carrie thought about trying to explain further but decided against it. She couldn't find the right words and, if she told Mr Wainwright that she had actually been quite frightened by her own outburst, she knew he wouldn't believe her.

'And don't walk back through the hall,' Mr Wainwright added. 'I think you've caused enough disturbance for one day. Walk round and through the school's main entrance. Perhaps the fresh air will clear your head and make you realize how stupidly you've behaved.'

Carrie did as she was told, trekking off along the path that ran around the perimeter of the school buildings until she reached the main entrance. She was beginning to feel angry with herself now. She walked in and headed straight for the detention room, slamming the door behind her in frustration.

She sat down at one of the desks near the back of the room, still furious that she had embarrassed herself so publicly. Carrie looked at the mood ring, expecting it to show red for the anger she was feeling.

But it was pink. The colour of optimism!

What do I have to be optimistic about? Carrie wondered. *A week of detention? People in school hating me for laughing during the minute's silence? The possibility of Lisa Jameson's little gang coming after me?* She stared mutinously at the ring. The colour was wrong. The ring was wrong. It was nothing but a stupid piece of junk!

In her anger, Carrie gripped the mood ring and tried to pull it off. It wouldn't move. No matter how hard she tugged at it, the ring remained firmly on her right index finger.

This just made Carrie all the more furious, and yet, even as she watched, the stone in the ring turned orange – orange for contentment.

Carrie shook her head, her breathing a little ragged now. *This isn't right*, she thought. *Why won't the ring come off?* She felt nervous, as though there was a part of her she couldn't control – the part of her that had laughed in assembly even though she hadn't wanted to. For fleeting seconds, ridiculous though she knew it was, Carrie blamed the ring.

She tried again to pull it free, and again it resisted her efforts. She swallowed hard and frowned at the mood ring. Then she heard footsteps heading towards the detention room and, moments later, Mrs Collet walked in, a furious expression on her face.

Despite the fact that she knew she was going to be told off again, Carrie was almost glad to see the head. At least the telling-off and the detention would take her mind off the ring for a while. And she was determined to take care of that, once and for all, when she got home.

'You're late,' Carrie heard her mum's voice say as she entered the house.

'I must be late if you're home before me,' Carrie joked, wandering into the kitchen.

'She's late because she had detention,' Mark smirked, looking up from the kitchen table where he was doing some homework.

'Why?' her mum asked. 'What happened?'

'I'll tell you later,' Carrie said. She crossed straight to the sink and rubbed some soap on her index finger, working the slippery lather all around the mood ring. The stone was shining red for anger. *That just proves it doesn't work,* Carrie thought. *I'm not feeling angry at all.*

'My meeting finished early,' her mum was saying. 'So I thought I'd come home and cook dinner for a change.'

Carrie nodded absently, her concentration focused on the ring. She began pulling at it, her finger now slippery with soap, but the irritating piece of jewellery remained stuck fast. She frowned in annoyance.

'What are you doing?' her mum asked curiously. 'Can I help?'

'I can do it,' Carrie snapped. Sighing in frustration, she wiped her hand on a piece of kitchen roll and walked across to the table where Mark was sitting.

Without hesitation she dug her fingertip into the butter and spread the yellow mess around her finger, taking care to work it underneath the mood ring.

'That's sick,' Mark said, watching her.

'Carrie, what are you trying to do?' Mrs Peterson demanded.

'I'm trying to get this stupid ring off,' Carrie retorted. 'But it won't move.'

'Do you want me to try?' her mum asked.

'I said I can do it,' Carrie blurted, feeling annoyed, but the ring remained on her finger as if welded there.

She wiped off the butter on a towel and hurried to the freezer, wrenching the door open.

'Now what?' Mark said, smiling.

'If my finger gets cold, it'll shrink,' Carrie told him. 'Then I'll be able to get the ring off.'

'That's stupid,' her mum said. 'Now close the freezer door.'

'Not until this ring's off,' Carrie said, defiantly. 'I must get it off. I've *got* to.'

'Carrie, you'll ruin the food that's in there. Close the door, please.'

'Besides, your hand might get frostbite and drop off,' Mark teased.

'Carrie, for goodness' sake, close the freezer door!' her mum insisted.

Carrie withdrew her hand and slammed the door in frustration. 'I'm not being silly,' she snapped. 'I just want this ring to come off.' She felt furious – why couldn't her family understand how important it was for her to get the ring off? She was trapped, like an animal in a cage – except that there was no cage, just a tiny metal band around one finger. A tiny metal band that wouldn't come off.

She looked around wildly for something else that she might be able to use to free the ring. Her gaze fell on her mother's porcelain vase standing on top of the freezer.

'Honestly, Carrie,' her mum was saying. 'I don't know what you're making so much fuss about. It's only a ring!'

Carrie felt like screaming. Instead, she snatched up the vase. 'And this is just an ornament,' she yelled, and threw it across the room.

It hit the far wall and shattered into a dozen pieces with a resounding *crash!* The silence that followed was deafening.

'That was my favourite vase,' her mum said quietly. 'Why did you do that?'

Carrie was already feeling guilty. Her anger had gone as quickly as it had come. She wanted to explain, but she didn't understand herself. She felt dizzy. Her head was full of conflicting thoughts. What was happening to her?

She looked at the horrified faces of her mother and brother. 'Mum . . .' she began, feeling drained of energy.

'Clear that mess up, please,' her mum said, a little sadly. 'Then I think you should go to your room and think about what you've done. All this fuss just because you can't get a ring off your finger. You're acting like a spoilt child!'

'I couldn't help it,' Carrie said pitifully. 'I don't know what's wrong. I've never had mood swings like this before.'

Her mum merely nodded and got on with the dinner.

Carrie crossed to the other side of the room,

where the broken pieces of the vase lay scattered across the floor. She bent slowly and reached for the first piece.

As she stretched out her hand she saw that the mood ring had changed colour again. It was yellow now. The colour of sickness. Instinctively, Carrie put one hand to her forehead, but she didn't seem to have a temperature. She wasn't ill. At least, she didn't think she was, and yet, as she pulled her shaking hand away, she saw that her skin was covered in a sheen of sweat.

She felt suddenly weak, and it seemed as if every muscle in her body ached. Her mouth filled with bile and she realized that she was going to be sick. Carrie jumped to her feet and ran for the downstairs cloakroom.

She made it just in time, and threw up in the toilet. Gasping for breath, she leaned back but, immediately, her stomach seemed to clench like a fist and she vomited again. She wiped her mouth with the back of her hand, her mind reeling. Sweat was pouring down her face, yet she felt as cold as ice. 'Carrie,' her mum said, appearing in the doorway, looking anxious.

Carrie nodded, unable to speak.

'Come on,' her mum said gently, trying to help her up. 'I didn't realize you were ill. Go on up to bed.'

Carrie waved away her mother's help. 'I can manage, thanks, Mum,' she gasped, relieved that the vomiting seemed to have stopped.

'Just go and rest,' her mum said. 'I'll bring you a cup of tea in a minute.'

'I just need to lie down for a moment,' Carrie replied. 'I'll come down when I feel better.' She put out a hand to get to her feet and saw that the ring was light blue – for happiness!

Oh, my God! Carrie thought. Right now, she wondered if she'd ever feel happy again.

She climbed the stairs slowly, aware that her mum was still standing in the hallway watching her. She was halfway up when the corners of her mouth began to lift in the same way they had that morning at school. She felt a smile spreading across her face, and immediately hurried up to her room and shut the door behind her so her mum wouldn't see.

She jumped on to her bed and buried her face in the pillow to muffle the laughter that was now beginning to spill from her – laughter over which she had no control.

For several minutes she lay there, laughing, until finally the hysterics began to subside. She sat up and looked at the ring. There had been the incident in assembly that morning, then the furious outburst in the kitchen, followed by sickness and now more uncontrollable laughter.

Don't even think it. It's impossible. Mad! Carrie told herself. But, no matter how mad it seemed, she could think of only one explanation: the ring had shown the appropriate colour just before each of the incidents had taken place. Instead of mirroring her moods, was the ring actually controlling them?

She shook her head, anxious to dismiss the ridiculous idea. But how else could she explain what had happened? Carrie sat on her bed, staring at the ring. Then she reached for her mobile and punched in her cousin Amy's number.

'Please be there, Amy,' Carrie said under her breath, listening to the phone ring.

'Hello?'

'Amy, it's me,' Carrie told her. 'I need to tell you something. I know it's going to sound crazy, but please just listen.'

When Carrie finally finished telling her cousin everything that had happened since she'd acquired the mood ring, there was nothing but silence on the other end of the phone.

'Amy, are you still there?' Carrie asked frantically.

'Yes, I'm just trying to work out what's going on,' Amy replied. 'So you think that the ring isn't reflecting your moods, it's creating them, right? You think the ring's controlling you?'

'I know it sounds mad but I don't know what else to think,' Carrie responded.

'It came off the front of a magazine you bought for ten pence, Carrie. How powerful can it be?' Amy said.

'I knew you wouldn't believe me,' Carrie sighed.

'I didn't say that. I just think it's a bit, well, far-fetched, that's all,' Amy told her.

'So do I, but I don't know how else to explain what's been happening to me. And, like I said, I can't get the wretched thing off!'

'Perhaps the best person to ask would be the old lady who ran the stall where you bought the magazine,' Amy suggested.

'But she doesn't even know I've got the ring,' Carrie pointed out.

'Well, go to the market and tell her. Talk to her. She might know something about it.'

'You think I'm mad, don't you, Amy?' Carrie asked.

'No. I think you're scared and confused,' Amy replied. 'And I think you should go and talk to the old lady, Carrie. The market's on today. I bet she'll be there. Call me again after you've spoken to her.'

Carrie took a deep breath. 'Thanks, Amy,' she said quietly, and hung up.

She pulled on a jacket and edged slowly out of her room. She could hear sounds of talking coming from the kitchen, and she knew that if she was going to get to the park she would have to sneak out of the house. Her mum would never let her out when she was ill.

Carrie crept quietly down the stairs, paused at the bottom, then tiptoed to the front door. She slipped out and closed the door as quietly as possible behind her, then she sprinted down the street. Instantly, she felt a little better. If the ring was dictating her moods, she was better off away from her family. If it made her angry again she was afraid of what she might do.

She ran faster, aware that the market would be closing soon. She didn't want to miss the old lady who'd sold her the magazine. As she ran, she felt her index finger throbbing, as if the ring was tightening its grip.

Carrie ran on, hurtling across the road without looking to see if there was any traffic coming. She felt herself shiver and wondered, for one terrible moment, if she was going to be sick again. She looked down at the ring. It was changing swiftly from yellow to brown. Just as rapidly, she felt confusion fill her head and, for a few seconds, she couldn't remember the way to the park. She skidded to a halt on a street corner and looked around in bewilderment. The feeling passed as the ring turned to light blue and Carrie hurried on.

There were some little children playing across the street and she saw one of them fall and land heavily on the pavement. He started to cry as his friends gathered around him, but Carrie could only laugh out loud at the sight.

At last she reached the park and dashed through the gates. The market was still open, so Carrie ran towards the site of the stall where she'd bought the magazine, but there was no sign of the old woman. Carrie looked around frantically, then hurried across to the stall opposite. There was a man there selling second-hand clothes. He was packing up.

'Excuse me,' Carrie said. 'Has the lady who runs the magazine and book stall been here today?'

The man shrugged. 'I suppose so,' he said, vaguely.

'You must have seen her,' Carrie snapped.

'Who do you mean?' he asked.

'She's old. She runs a stall that sells second-hand books and old magazines.'

'There's a couple of stalls like that here,' he replied, unhelpfully.

'She means Four-Fingered Lily,' said the man on the next-door stall selling board games. He looked at Carrie. 'Don't you, love?'

'Is that her name?' Carrie asked.

He nodded. 'She's been coming here for years,' the man with the board games said. 'Longer than I have, I reckon.'

'Do you know where she is? I need to speak to her,' Carrie begged.

'You've just missed her. She packed up about five minutes ago.'

'Which way did she go?' Carrie demanded frantically. 'Please tell me.'

The man nodded towards the park's other entrance.

Carrie was about to turn and run in that direction when a thought struck her. 'Why is she called that?' she asked the games seller. 'Four-fingered Lily?'

'Because she's missing a finger, love,' he smiled. 'Why do you think?'

Carrie set off as fast as she could. She scanned the pathways of the park, and suddenly spotted a figure pushing a supermarket trolley full of cardboard boxes. She set off after the old lady and caught up with her at last.

'I have to speak to you,' Carrie panted.

'What about?' the old lady said, still pushing the trolley along.

'About this,' Carrie said, raising her right index finger and brandishing it in front of the old lady like a weapon.

'You said you wanted it, but I wouldn't let you have it!' the old lady exclaimed, stopping in surprise. 'Where did you get it from?'

'I found it on the ground,' Carrie told her. 'But you knew about it, didn't you? That's why you didn't want me to have it,' she went on.

'Girls! They can never resist a pretty piece of jewellery. I was the same when I was your age,' said the old lady, shaking her head. Suddenly, she spun round to face Carrie, pulling her own right hand from inside her coat pocket and holding it out.

Carrie stared. The index finger of the old lady's right hand was missing. There was little more than a stump where the digit should have been.

'I was like you,' said the woman. 'I saw a mood ring and I wanted it and I got it. Along with things I didn't want. That was why I got rid of it.' She tapped the stump of her index finger. 'The trouble was, the ring didn't want to go.' She thrust the stump towards Carrie. 'It was the only way to get rid of the ring. And if you've got any sense, you'll do the same. Before it's too late,' she finished, pushing her trolley on again.

'What do you mean "Before it's too late"?' Carrie called after her.

'You already know what I mean,' the old lady said, over her shoulder. 'You know what must be done.'

Carrie stood alone, watching as the old lady walked away. For a moment she felt faint, and feared she was going to pass out, but the feeling subsided and she turned for home. She went a little slower this time, not sure what she was going to say when she got back. How was she going to explain to her mum and dad what she'd just heard? They would never believe her about the ring.

As Carrie walked, the old lady's words echoed inside her head: *'You know what must be done.'*

* * *

'Where have you been? I thought you were ill. You were supposed to be resting in your room!' Mrs Peterson said, as Carrie walked into the house.

Carrie burst into tears. It happened so suddenly even she was surprised. She ran to her mum who threw both arms around her and hugged her.

'What's wrong, love?' her mum asked.

'I've got to get this ring off, Mum,' Carrie sobbed, holding up her right index finger.

'I don't blame you, it's a tacky piece of jewellery,' Mrs Peterson remarked.

'No, you don't understand. It's been doing things to me. Making me feel things I don't want to feel. Making me *act* in ways I don't want to act.'

'Don't be silly, love. It's just a ring,' her mum said firmly.

'Just help me get it off. *Please!*' Carrie shrieked. 'There's something wrong with it.'

Mrs Peterson shook her head. 'You can be such a drama queen at times,' she said, stroking Carrie's hair. 'But, come on, if I can help you get that silly old ring off, I will.' She led Carrie into the kitchen just as the phone rang in the living-room. Mrs Peterson gave Carrie a hug and went to answer it.

'You know what must be done.' Carrie heard the old woman's voice in her head. *'Before it's too late.'*

Still sobbing, she looked down at the ring. It was yellow for sickness. She felt a stabbing pain in her stomach and looked around frantically for something to help her get the ring off. She could see nothing she hadn't already tried, so she gripped the ring and twisted it on her finger, desperate to remove it.

She got it as far as the knuckle, twisting and pulling at it madly until her skin was red and sore. She continued to tug at it despite the pain but it would go no further. Carrie tried once more, the edge of the ring actually cutting into her flesh so that blood began to run down her finger.

'You know what must be done.'

Carrie was crying as she pulled open the kitchen drawer and grabbed the largest, sharpest knife. It was the only answer, but she was terrified. The ring glowed purple.

Blinking away her tears, she rested her right index finger on the edge of the kitchen sink and grasped the knife firmly in her left hand. Then she rested the razor-sharp edge of the blade against her index finger, just below the ring.

'Do it. Cut the finger off and get rid of the ring!' she told herself. She gritted her teeth, but she was shaking so much she could barely keep her grip on the knife.

The mood ring was still purple.

Carrie took a deep breath and tried to steel herself. She pressed a little harder on the blade, wondering if she would faint before she actually managed to cut off her finger.

Do it! Before it's too late! she thought, and prepared to bring all her weight down on the knife.

'NO!' Mrs Peterson screamed, cannoning into Carrie and sending the knife flying out of her hand. 'What are you doing?' her mother shrieked.

The knife skittered across the floor and Carrie scrambled after it, trying to grab it and hack off her finger before her mother could stop her.

But her mum also made a grab for the knife. 'Carrie,' she shouted, 'stop it!' And she pushed Carrie hard in an effort to keep her away from the blade.

Carrie fell backwards, her arms pin-wheeling. Her head slammed hard against the kitchen wall. There was a moment's pain. Then darkness.

The light was blinding. So white and brilliant in its intensity that Carrie could barely open her eyes. When she finally did, she saw that the walls of the room she was in were the same brilliant white. So was the bed-linen and the long nightdress that she wore. She swung herself out of bed and took a couple of steps across the room.

She tried to remember what had happened. In her mind's eye, she saw the struggle with her mum in the kitchen. She saw the knife too.

The memories flooded back. She looked down at her right hand. The ring was still there on her index finger. It showed light blue. Happiness.

Carrie felt her face break into a smile, but it was a gesture over which she had absolutely no control. She didn't feel happy, far from it, but her smile wouldn't fade. Not even when she got to her feet, walked over to the cold metal door and pulled at the handle, only to find that it wouldn't open. It was locked.

There was a small opening in the door that looked like a letterbox with glass across it. She peered through the slot, then stepped back hurriedly as some people approached and unlocked the door.

She didn't recognize the man in the white coat who walked in first. Her parents followed him into the room, looking upset and anxious. Carrie wanted to get up and run to them, but she didn't move.

'Carrie,' the doctor said, softly.

She began to laugh. A high-pitched, frenzied laugh that she couldn't suppress.

'It's the same every time we speak to her,' the man told her parents. 'We can't get a word out of her. She's been like this ever since she was brought in to the hospital. I've worked in psychiatry for twelve years now and I've never seen a case quite like this one.'

Carrie opened her mouth to speak, annoyed that the man was talking about her as if she wasn't there. She wanted to tell her mum and dad how much she loved them. She wanted them to take her away from this strange, white place. But she couldn't. She could only laugh, the infernal sound reverberating off the walls, mocking and spiteful. The only sound Carrie could make. The only sound she would ever hear. Now, and for the rest of her life.

'Go on, Brandon, keep climbing, you're almost there,' Brandon Taylor heard his brother, Jake, shout encouragingly from down below. With one last, huge effort, Brandon heaved himself up on to the top of the high stone wall and sat astride it, peering down triumphantly at Jake.

He could see his identical twin standing with his hands on his hips, gazing up at him.

'Come on, then!' Brandon called down. 'Slow

coach!' He watched as Jake reached for the ladder and propped it against the wall, checking it was secure before beginning his own ascent.

'Why couldn't I have used the ladder too?' Brandon asked as his brother reached the top of the wall.

'You said you could climb up by yourself,' Jake reminded him, swinging a leg over so that he too was sitting safely astride the cold stone. 'Anyway, I'm carrying the paint and the brushes, aren't I?' He set a tin of black emulsion and two large paint brushes down on top of the wall between them.

Brandon looked out across the garden that lay beyond the wall. 'No wonder Great-aunt Lucy doesn't want anyone to see in here,' he mused, gazing at the overgrown wilderness that stretched away before him. 'It doesn't look as if she's done any gardening for years!'

Jake nodded in agreement, also surveying the expanse of land.

Brandon looked down to the bottom of the wall.

Beneath them were several overgrown lilac bushes, their branches intertwined like battling squids. Ivy covered the stone the boys sat on, clinging on to it like clutching fingers. Brandon rattled a length of it experimentally. It was tough and strong, he noted with approval. It could be a useful tool in the climb down.

Beyond the lilac bushes and untended flower-beds a large expanse of overgrown lawn stretched away towards a line of willow and poplar trees that masked the bottom part of the garden from the house itself.

The building was just visible through the branches of the trees. It was a huge Tudor mansion that looked only slightly better cared for than the garden that surrounded it. Paint was peeling badly from the outside walls, the tiled roof was clearly missing some slates and a nearby outhouse had pieces of reed sticking out of its thatched roof like badly combed hair.

'No wonder nobody ever comes here,' Brandon

said, dismissing the ivy and deciding to use the ladder to get down. He heaved it up from the outside of the wall and lowered it into the garden. 'The house looks as bad as its grounds.'

'That's not why people don't come here, though,' Jake pointed out. 'It's because of Great-aunt Lucy. The kids in the village are scared of her.'

'I'm not surprised. She's a miserable old bat.'

'And rude,' Jake added.

'And mean,' Brandon laughed.

'It's just a pity she's our great-aunt,' Jake said with a sigh.

'Perhaps if she spent more time talking to people instead of staring through that telescope of hers every night, more people would come and visit her,' Brandon said, starting to climb down the ladder.

'By the time we've finished she won't be spending much time looking out of that window,' Jake grinned.

'At least, not unless she's got X-ray eyes and she

can see through the paint we're going to use on the glass,' Brandon agreed with a chuckle.

'I heard that she wasn't *always* as weird as she is now,' Jake said. 'She just went a bit, well, mad, after her twin sister disappeared years ago.'

'Where did she go?' Brandon asked curiously.

'No one knows, you twit. If they did she wouldn't still be missing, would she?' Jake told him, laughing.

Brandon had to acknowledge the truth of that. He grinned. 'Hey, tell you what, she probably just got fed up with Great-aunt Lucy and ran away,' he said, jumping down from the ladder and landing in the tangled grass.

'Here, take the paint,' Jake called, leaning forward and throwing the can carefully to Brandon.

Brandon caught it, then watched as Jake stuck the two paint-brushes in the back pocket of his jeans and quickly climbed down the ladder to join him.

Brandon took the paint, Jake carried the ladder

and the two of them set off across the lawn towards the line of trees, pausing when they got there to check that the coast was clear. The house was close now, across another stretch of unmown lawn and a weed-infested gravel pathway.

Brandon checked that there was no sign of his great-aunt, then led the way over to the house. He passed a pond, its surface covered with thick green slime. It was surrounded by several statues and he couldn't help noticing that one had its head missing.

Brandon stopped behind a large hydrangea bush that was growing close to the house. Jake almost bumped into him.

'So which room is the one with the telescope?' Jake wanted to know, peering up at the house from the cover of the bush.

'Shhh,' Brandon warned. 'Keep your voice down or she'll hear us coming.' He pointed to one of the first-floor windows. 'She keeps the telescope in that room up there, I think. But we'll do one or two of the others as well, just to make sure.' He laughed. 'She's going to think it's a bit dark tonight when she looks through her telescope. I wonder how long it'll take her to realize her windows are covered in black paint!'

Jake chuckled and prized the lid off the paint tin while Brandon pushed the ladder up against the wall of the house.

Brandon took the tin of paint and a brush from Jake and climbed the ladder. He peeped cautiously through the window to make sure Great-aunt Lucy wasn't in that very room and then dipped the brush into the black paint.

'Go on,' Jake urged impatiently. 'I'll do the next one.'

Brandon was about to press the brush to the glass when a loud yapping nearly made him fall off the ladder.

'Oh no, I'd forgotten about Michelangelo!' said Jake, as a small brown and white spaniel hurtled towards him.

Barking and growling, the little dog ran at Jake, who promptly climbed up the ladder behind Brandon.

'What are you doing?' Brandon demanded. 'Get down!'

'I don't want to get bitten!' Jake explained, staying put.

'Great-aunt Lucy's got more teeth than that dog,' Brandon told him. 'Just go and stroke him, calm him down, otherwise she might hear him barking.'

'*You* calm him down,' Jake said indignantly, staring down at the little dog who was still yapping excitedly up at the boys, his tail wagging furiously.

'Oh, get on with it!' Brandon snapped. 'We can't stay up here all day. Look, he likes you, his tail's wagging.'

Slowly, Jake descended the ladder. 'Good dog, Michelangelo,' he said nervously. The dog stopped yapping and jumped up at Jake eagerly. Jake patted him gently on the head and Michelangelo bounced around his legs in excitement – and bumped against the foot of the ladder.

The ladder shifted and Brandon let out a cry of surprise and alarm as he wobbled uncertainly for a moment. 'I'm going to fall,' he yelled.

As Jake tried to draw Michelangelo away from the ladder, the little dog bumped into it once again. This time, Brandon clutched the windowsill to steady himself and dropped the tin of paint.

It fell to the ground and landed with a thud. Black paint sprayed in all directions, most of it over the patio, but some up the wall of the house. Several thick black blobs landed on Michelangelo, who promptly squealed and fled around the side of the house, yelping.

'Uh-oh,' said Jake, looking at the spreading puddle of black paint. 'Let's get out of here. Quick!'

Brandon dropped the paint-brush and scrambled down the ladder as fast as he could, jumping the last three rungs. No sooner had he hit the ground than he heard an angry voice cutting through the warm summer air.

'What do you think you're doing?'

Great-aunt Lucy had appeared around one corner of the house, shaking her pudgy fist angrily at the boys. For an old lady she moved with surprising speed.

'Run!' Brandon yelled, racing away from his great-aunt towards the front of the house, with Jake close on his heels.

'How dare you?' Great-aunt Lucy bellowed, giving chase as the boys fled down the long gravel driveway that led from the great house, then frantically climbed the gate. 'You won't get away with this, you know!'

But Brandon didn't stop. Glancing over his shoulder, he saw that his great-aunt had given up the chase. Instead she stood outside the house, with Michelangelo leaping about her ankles, yapping excitedly. 'You'll be sorry!' she shouted after him furiously.

* * *

'I can't believe you'd do something so stupid,' Mr Taylor snapped.

Brandon didn't know what to say. He could see by the way his dad was striding out that he was not happy. He looked hopefully at his brother, who was trailing along behind. Jake shrugged. Clearly he didn't have any bright ideas or brilliant excuses either.

'I mean, you're thirteen,' their dad continued. 'You're not little kids any more.'

'Dad, we were only having a bit of a joke,' Jake said sheepishly.

'A joke?' his dad snapped. 'Vandalizing your great-aunt's house is a joke, is it?'

'We didn't vandalize it, Dad,' Brandon put in. 'And anyway, we were just going to paint a couple of the windows black for a laugh . . .'

'I know what you were going to do. Your great-aunt said she found the paint spilled all over the patio.'

'Sorry, Dad,' Brandon muttered, just as Jake said exactly the same thing.

'Well, that's not good enough this time,' Mr Taylor said. 'I know you two can find trouble even when you're not looking for it, but this is disgraceful! You were trespassing on your great-aunt's land. You were going to paint over her windows. And as if that isn't bad enough, you could have hurt yourselves. You're lucky one of you didn't fall off that ladder! What you did was dangerous, irresponsible and downright stupid. How on earth did you expect to get away with it? Did you think your own great-aunt wouldn't recognize you? She rang me as soon as you two had run off.'

'If it hadn't been for the dog—' Brandon began.

'You'd have painted over her windows!' Mr Taylor interrupted. 'You'd have had your little joke and got away with it! And did you ever stop to think about how your great-aunt would have felt if your little prank had succeeded? Apart from her dog, she's all on her own in that big house with no one to talk to. She's just a lonely old lady who's been unhappy ever since her sister went missing when they were both ten. That was fifty-five years ago.' Mr Taylor sighed as they crossed the road that led out of the village towards Great-aunt Lucy's house. 'Well, I'm going to let your great-aunt decide what you two can do to make this up to her. If I was her, I'd make you clean the entire house from top to bottom.'

Jake groaned. 'That'd take forever, Dad,' he said. 'I don't think that place has been dusted for about ten years!'

'That's because your great-aunt can't get about too well these days,' said Mr Taylor.

'She was moving quickly enough when she came running out of her house to chase us,' Brandon remarked, and instantly wished he hadn't.

His dad glared at him and Brandon bowed his head. He'd never seen his dad so angry before. 'Sorry, Dad,' he said again.

'You can apologize to your great-aunt,' Mr Taylor

told them as he unlocked the gate into Great-aunt Lucy's driveway.

Brandon glanced quickly across at his brother and met Jake's gaze. He knew that Jake was dreading this as much as he was.

They stood, silent and uncomfortable, as their dad strode up to the front door and banged three times with the large, lion-headed brass knocker. Brandon thought that the face of the metal lion seemed to be leering mockingly at him.

After a moment or two the door opened and Great-aunt Lucy looked out. She smiled at the boys' dad then looked at the twins and raised her eyebrows questioningly.

'Well, I've brought these two reprobates to see you,' said Mr Taylor. 'They'd like to say sorry for their stupid prank earlier.'

'Sorry,' Brandon and Jake piped up together.

'And they'd like to do something to help you, wouldn't you, boys?' Mr Taylor continued.

Brandon and Jake nodded unenthusiastically.

'So, whatever you want them to do, just let them know and they'll get on with it,' Mr Taylor finished.

Great-aunt Lucy nodded. 'Very well. Thank you,' she said. 'You'd better come inside, boys,' she added, frostily.

As Brandon headed past his dad towards Great-aunt Lucy, Mr Taylor bent to whisper in his ear.

'I don't want to see you two back home until you've finished whatever job your great-aunt sets you doing,' he said sharply. 'Understand?'

'Yes, Dad,' Brandon replied miserably.

As he entered the house, he heard his dad's feet crunching on the gravel as he strode away.

Brandon watched apprehensively as Great-aunt Lucy shut the front door behind him, then ambled off towards a room on her left. He and Jake stayed put in the hall, gazing around warily.

'It's like a museum in here,' Jake whispered. 'It's even dustier than I remembered.'

'Well, it must be a couple of years since we've been here,' Brandon reminded him.

'Come here, boys,' Great-aunt Lucy called, and the twins wandered unenthusiastically in the direction of her voice.

She was standing in front of a large open fireplace in her living-room. The room was huge – so huge that the high ceiling made the slightest noise echo and, when Great-aunt Lucy coughed, the sound seemed to bounce around the room like a tennis ball. Brandon noticed that inside the fireplace, instead of wood or coal, there was a metal container filled with flowers. Their scent filled the room with a sweet, cloying fragrance that made him feel slightly sick. There was a worn, gold-coloured three-piece suite and several ornate table lamps. Brandon looked down at his feet and noticed that the gold carpet was worn so thin in places that the wooden floorboards beneath it were showing through.

The walls were festooned with paintings of all sorts, from portraits to landscapes. The twins' mother was a history teacher, so Brandon was able to recognize one of them as the Battle of Waterloo. Cobwebs clung to most of the frames. But the paintings served a useful purpose, for the walls behind them were in a terrible state. The plasterwork was chipped and, in a number of places, had actually crumbled away from the wall entirely. Brandon could see some of it lying in the fireplace, looking like chunks of crushed meringue.

'Since I spoke to your father earlier, I have been trying to think of a job you can do for me,' Great-aunt Lucy said. 'I considered asking you to weed the garden or even clean the windows, but then I decided that, as you both seem to be so fond of painting, I would ask you to do some decorating for me.'

Brandon and Jake exchanged a look of despair. If the rest of the house was anything like the living-room, then Brandon didn't even want to imagine what kind of job lay in store for them.

'Follow me,' said Great-aunt Lucy, leading the

way out into the hall. She paused to ensure that the boys were behind her and then began to climb the wide staircase.

There were more paintings on the walls that lined the stairs. Here they partially concealed poorly hung, discoloured wallpaper that was covered in a hideous flowery pattern. The stairs creaked as they climbed and Brandon could see dust swirling in the sunshine that streamed in through a large landing window.

There were six doors leading off the landing, one of which was down a short, dark corridor to the right. It was that door towards which Great-aunt Lucy led the boys. Brandon was struck by the fact that the door opened smoothly and easily, as if on well-oiled hinges. Given the neglected air of the rest of the house, he had been expecting a protesting squeak.

'In here,' Great-aunt Lucy said, motioning them inside.

The room was empty. There wasn't even a carpet

on the floor, just bare boards beneath their feet. The door swung smoothly shut behind them with the faintest sigh and Brandon felt a breath of air on the back of his neck. He shivered uneasily.

'Did you feel that?' he asked Jake, glancing at his brother. 'It was as if somebody just blew on the back of my neck.'

Jake shrugged; clearly he'd felt nothing unusual. Brandon figured that he was letting his imagination run away with him in the creepy old house.

'I want you to strip the wallpaper,' Great-aunt Lucy was saying. 'As you can see, the room needs redecorating. It hasn't been touched for more than fifty years.'

'No kidding,' Brandon murmured.

'What did you say, Brandon?' his great-aunt asked sharply.

'Nothing, Great-aunt Lucy,' he said quickly, giving her a bright smile.

'I'll go and fetch you what you need,' she continued. 'A bucket of warm water, some sponges and some knives should be just the thing to get this paper down.'

Both boys nodded as the old lady moved out of the room.

'I think a flame-thrower might be more useful,' Brandon remarked, looking at the lumpy, discoloured paper that covered all four walls. It was a deep red colour, traced with silver lines that rippled across it like glistening veins. He ran his fingers over it experimentally. It was thick and felt more like fabric than paper. It also seemed to be pretty firmly attached to the wall.

'We could do with Dad's steamer,' Jake agreed, joining Brandon at the nearest wall. 'That'd get it off more quickly than knives and hot water will.' He prodded the wallpaper. 'This stuff looks like it was put up with concrete.'

Suddenly, the door of the room swung shut and, again, Brandon heard what sounded like a faint sigh. A shiver ran swiftly up and down his spine. He turned round but there was no one and nothing behind him, so he returned his attention to the wall.

'I could run home and get the steamer,' Jake suggested. 'Or shall we try with the water and knives first?'

Brandon nodded, without looking at his brother. He wasn't really listening, for the wall fascinated him and he was suddenly gripped by a huge curiosity to see what lay behind the paper.

'Brandon,' Jake persisted. 'I said I could run—'

'. . . home, and get the steamer,' Brandon finished for him. 'Yes, I know. It's a good idea. Wait until the old girl's brought the water and the rest of the stuff, and then you can sneak out and get it.'

'How long do you reckon the paper's been up?' Jake asked.

'I don't know. A long time by the look of it,' Brandon told him.

He heard movement outside the door and turned to see Great-aunt Lucy coming in, carrying a bucket of water with two sponges floating in it. She took two putty knives from the pocket of her cardigan and handed one to each boy.

'There's a stepladder out on the landing,' Great-aunt Lucy said. 'You can use that to reach the tops of the walls.'

Brandon nodded as his great-aunt frowned at him and left the room.

'I'll get started,' Brandon said with a sigh, reaching for one of the sponges in the bucket. 'You go and get the steamer.'

'OK,' Jake said. 'Back in a minute.' And he hurried out, closing the door behind him.

Brandon pressed the wet sponge against a section of the wallpaper nearest to him, and watched as the fluid ran down the paper. Then he picked at the edge of the wallpaper strip to see how easily it would come away from the wall. The paper peeled back a little way and, as Brandon touched the wall behind it, he was surprised by how cold it felt. A chill ran through his fingers, up his arm and down his back like some weird kind of freezing electric shock.

Once again he heard the low whisper of a sigh that had signalled the opening and closing of the door. He looked round, expecting to see that Great-aunt Lucy had returned and readying himself to explain Jake's absence. But the door was closed.

When Jake got back to the room with the steamer, his brother was pleased to see him. Stripping the wallpaper with a wet sponge and a putty knife was slow going, although Brandon had actually made some decent headway.

Work progressed much more speedily, however, with the help of the steamer. The room, which had already smelled musty, was soon filled with thick, stifling steam, but Jake worked hard, determined to get the job over with as soon as possible.

Before long, the first strip of ancient wallpaper began to peel away from the wall next to the door. Like the wilting petal of some dying flower, it drooped then fell slowly to the floor. Standing on top of the stepladder, Jake cheered, but the sound caught in his throat as he saw what was behind the paper.

Instead of bare and patchy plaster, part of a fabulous painting had been revealed. Its colours were surprisingly vivid and, in the drab, steamy old room, it was the very last thing Jake had been expecting to see. The painting appeared to depict a group of men in fancy, old-fashioned clothes, with white ruffs around their necks, standing beside horses in a lush green field. Behind them, rolling hills stretched away towards the horizon under a clear, cloudless, brilliantly blue sky.

Brandon, who had just opened one of the windows to let the worst of the steam out, turned back at the sound of Jake's stifled cheer. He stood motionless, staring at the painting in amazement as Jake climbed slowly down the stepladder to join him. They both gazed silently for a moment at what they had uncovered.

Then Jake stepped forward, fascinated by the picture that lay behind the paper. 'It's a mural, not a framed picture,' he remarked, touching the tableau gently. 'It's actually painted on the wall itself.'

'Can you tell what time period it's supposed to be?' Brandon asked, his eyes never leaving the wall.

Jake shrugged. 'I don't know,' he said thoughtfully. 'They're wearing very old-fashioned clothes. They look kind of Elizabethan. Mum did say that this house is Elizabethan.'

'So you think the painting's been here for, like, four hundred years?' Brandon queried. 'I'm not so sure. The colours are really bright. I'd have thought that after four hundred years they would have faded more than this.'

'Perhaps it's because the picture's been covered by this thick wallpaper for so long,' Jake suggested. 'Or it might not be four hundred years old at all. The paper can't have been up that long. Perhaps the painting was only done fifty or sixty years ago. That might be why the colours are still so vivid.'

Brandon nodded. 'He doesn't look too happy,

does he?' he commented, pointing towards a figure in the foreground.

It was a boy who looked to be roughly the same age as Jake and Brandon. He was dressed in the same Elizabethan clothes as the men in the picture. However, unlike the men, who were looking at their horses, his painted face was staring out of the picture right at the twins, and the expression on it was one of complete fear and disbelief.

Jake was studying the boy curiously when Brandon interrupted his thoughts.

'I wonder what that means,' Brandon said, pointing to a gold border that ran along the top of the mural. It bore a phrase that appeared to be written in a foreign language.

'*"Fatum tuum, nisi celata fuerit pictura, idem erit"*,' Jake read aloud.

'It isn't French or Spanish,' Brandon went on. 'I don't recognize the words from anything we've done in school.'

'Maybe it's Latin,' Jake mused. 'I mean, if the

painting was done in Elizabethan times then that would make sense. They wrote in Latin back then, didn't they?'

'I think so,' Brandon replied. 'I wonder if there's more of the mural on the rest of the wall.' He started pulling at another piece of damp wallpaper.

Jake ran the steamer over this next section and between them the boys worked the strip of wallpaper free.

'Wow!' gasped Brandon.

The blue sky that featured in the first part of the mural remained the same, as did the brilliant green landscape forming the backdrop. However, where there'd been a small group of men in the first section, the next part showed hundreds of them.

'It's a battle scene,' Jake said in fascination, looking at the clusters of soldiers on foot and on horseback. 'But these guys look different.' He was intrigued by the fact that the opposing forces were dressed differently from each other, and there wasn't a ruff in sight – on either side. One side in the battle wore thick buff jackets and steel helmets, but their opposition, particularly the cavalry, were more gaudily dressed. Many sported large feathers in their hats.

'It looks like something from the English Civil War,' Brandon noted.

'So the first section is Elizabethan,' Jake added, racking his brains to try and remember when the English Civil War had been. 'But the English Civil War was later, wasn't it?'

'Yeah,' Brandon confirmed. 'I remember Mum saying it was sixteen forty-something.'

'So this second section is showing something that happened over fifty years after the first section,' Jake remarked. He looked up. 'And there's more Latin writing over the top of it, too.'

'I wonder if the same artist did it all,' Brandon said thoughtfully.

'Maybe,' Jake replied. 'Maybe a modern artist did the whole thing.'

'Which side do you think she was on?' Brandon

wanted to know. He was looking at the figure of a girl in the foreground of the latest section of the painting.

Jake stared at her curiously. It was hard to tell which side she was on because she didn't seem interested in the battle at all. Like the boy in the first part of the mural, she was the only one to be looking out of the painting, and, like the boy, there was an expression of fear on her face.

Eagerly, Jake and Brandon stripped more of the paper from the walls and found that the battle scene stretched another half metre or so across the mural.

'The colours are still bright,' Brandon remarked. 'Just like in the first section.'

Jake nodded. 'I wonder if Great-aunt Lucy knows that this mural's here,' he mused. 'If the paper was put up fifty-odd years ago, she'd only have been a little girl at the time.'

'Why don't you go and ask her?' Brandon suggested. 'And while you're down there, ask her if we can have a drink, too. All this steam has made me thirsty.'

'I'm not going,' Jake protested, not particularly keen to go and talk to his great-aunt.

'One of us has got to. I'll do you Scissors-Paper-Stone to decide,' Brandon said.

Jake nodded and hid one hand behind his back.

'Ready,' said Brandon. 'One, two, three . . .'

Jake whipped his hand into view and groaned as Brandon did the same. Jake had gone for paper. Brandon had chosen scissors.

'I win!' Brandon grinned. 'Scissors cut paper.'

'Best of three?' Jake suggested hopefully, but the look on Brandon's face said it all. Jake turned and headed out of the room, as his brother turned back to uncover more of the mural.

Brandon ran the steamer over the next section of wallpaper, but it was stubborn and showed no sign of coming loose. Brandon sighed and reached for his putty knife. He slid it underneath the edge of the paper, prying it carefully away from the wall beneath.

Gradually the strip came free and Brandon pulled it down, exposing a little more of the mural. Another strip soon followed as Brandon worked to uncover another section of the painting. He stepped back to look at the latest portion.

Once again the clothes of the figures had changed. There was a small group of men who were standing together on the brilliant green hillside. They wore black shirts and tall black hats.

'Puritans,' murmured Brandon, recognizing the strange hats from pictures he'd seen at school. He reckoned that again, the mural was showing a period some years later than the last.

He felt something warm on his fingers and guessed it was some wallpaper glue. He frowned when he looked down to see that it was blood. Quickly he glanced at the blade of the putty knife and saw that there were two tiny specks of blood on that too.

Had he cut himself? Brandon didn't see how he could have done, the blade was too blunt. It barely cut through the paper. He wiped the blood on his jeans and examined his hands. Then he shook his head in bewilderment: he had no cuts on his fingers.

Brandon shrugged and looked back to the mural again – and what he saw made him feel as if his entire body had been dipped in ice water.

There was a figure in the foreground as there had been in all the other sections of the mural. And, just as in those other sections, this figure was looking directly out of the painting. It was a boy of about thirteen, dressed in Puritan clothes. Both his hands were raised above his head as if he was surrendering, and the palm of his right hand bore a small, deep cut. Brandon could see the red of blood splashed across it.

He touched it with the tip of his index finger and it felt warm. Just like blood. He shivered uneasily. *The steamer must have caused the paint on the mural to run*, he told himself firmly. Yes, that had to be the answer.

He was still standing looking at the mural when the door of the room opened and Jake came in carrying two glasses of orange juice.

'I got our drinks,' Jake said triumphantly, handing a glass to his brother.

Brandon took a sip of his orange juice, but continued to gaze at the boy in the mural and the cut on his palm. He glanced down again at the blade of the putty knife.

'Great-aunt Lucy said we can help ourselves to orange juice from the fridge,' Jake went on. 'She's not that bad really, you know.'

Brandon nodded blankly, still immersed in contemplation of the mural.

'Are you all right?' Jake asked, putting one hand on his brother's arm.

'I uncovered another piece of the mural,' Brandon told him. 'It's a scene from after the English Civil War was over.'

'Yeah, great,' Jake said, reaching for something in his back pocket. 'But look what I found while I was downstairs.'

'I wonder who they are,' Brandon said, gazing at the girls in the small, framed, black and white photograph that his brother held out.

'I saw the picture in the kitchen when I was getting our drinks,' Jake said. 'Don't you recognize them?' He jabbed a finger at the girls in the picture. They were about ten years old, wearing dresses with their hair in long pigtails. 'Look at her face.' Jake pointed to the girl on the right of the picture. 'I think it's Great-aunt Lucy with her twin sister – the one who went missing. There are more pictures of them both downstairs.'

'Oh my God. You'd better put it back, Jake,' Brandon said anxiously. 'If Great-aunt Lucy sees this is missing we might end up with another punishment!'

'Don't stress. I'll do it later,' Jake said, stuffing the picture back into his jeans pocket. 'She won't notice anyway, she's outside in the garden.'

'What was that noise?' Brandon asked, suddenly spinning around.

'I didn't hear anything,' Jake replied, frowning.

'Listen,' Brandon told him.

Jake stood still in the steamy room, watching Brandon. After a moment, Brandon heard a slight rustling sound, not loud enough to be floorboards. It reminded him more of fingertips sliding across paper.

'Look,' Brandon snapped, pointing towards the far wall of the room. 'It's moving,' he said. 'The paper's moving!'

'There must be air bubbles trapped underneath it,' Jake suggested, watching as the paper undulated gently.

Then, one by one, four small bulges began to appear in the paper, close to each other. To Brandon they looked like fingertips. It was almost as if someone was pressing against the wallpaper from the other side. 'Air bubbles,'

Brandon repeated, in an effort to reassure himself more than Jake.

'Come on,' Jake insisted, reaching for the steamer. 'Let's get the rest of the paper off the walls. I want to see what else is on this mural.'

Time had lost all meaning for Brandon. He was only interested in tearing the wallpaper down and uncovering the rest of the mural. He knew that he and Jake had been working for several hours, but he didn't care.

'Can't we pack it in for today?' Jake asked. 'I'm sure Great-aunt Lucy won't mind if we come back and finish up tomorrow.'

Brandon ignored him; in fact, he hardly heard him. He was too immersed in stripping away more of the paper.

'Brandon, I said, let's leave it until tomorrow, eh? I'm worn out,' Jake tried again.

Brandon ignored him once more. He didn't want to stop and he was hoping that if he didn't respond Jake would just shut up about it.

'Brandon,' Jake groaned insistently.

Brandon sighed. Clearly he was going to have to answer. 'I'm not leaving it,' he snapped.

Jake sighed but did not protest. However, while Jake stopped for a rest every now and then, Brandon kept on working away with the steamer and his putty knife, tearing off strips of the old paper and gazing in awe at each fresh section of the mural that was exposed. In every case the colours of the painting looked as bright and brilliant as the day they had first been applied to the wall.

He was particularly fascinated by the fact that as he worked his way around the room, the times depicted in the mural were changing, becoming closer to the present day. As Brandon tore another strip away, he was sure that the figures in the latest section were decked out in finest Georgian splendour.

Brandon stepped back from the wall to the centre of the room and looked around at what had been uncovered so far. Three walls had now been stripped to reveal the secrets beneath. Closest to the door was the Elizabethan scene then, moving clockwise, the other tableaux followed.

'There's no way this was done by the same artist if each scene was painted during the period it shows,' Brandon said thoughtfully. 'The artist would have to have been two hundred years old at least!'

'Yes,' Jake agreed. 'I guess this was either created by separate artists or a modern painter did the whole thing.'

'The style's the same in every section. So is the background,' Brandon pointed out. 'That means it was probably all done by one artist.'

'And there's one of those frightened figures looking out of the painting in every different historical period,' Jake agreed.

'It would have taken one artist ages to paint all this,' Brandon murmured.

'Not *two hundred years* though,' Jake grinned. 'But,

look, that Latin sentence is repeated above each section,' he added. 'I'd love to know what it means.'

'Yeah, but we don't know anybody who speaks Latin,' Brandon pointed out. 'There's no way we can find out what it means.'

Jake's eyes lit up. 'Yes there is,' he said, smiling. 'I could key it into a translation site on the internet.'

'And how are you going to do that? I don't see Great-aunt Lucy owning a computer,' Brandon replied.

'Well, let's take a break, go home and do it there,' Jake suggested. 'It won't take long.'

'You go,' Brandon told him, strangely unwilling to leave the mural. 'I'll keep going here.'

Jake gave him an odd look. 'Are you sure? Why don't you come with me? Great-aunt Lucy won't mind.'

'I said I'll keep working!' Brandon snapped. He saw a look of concern cross Jake's face and realized he'd been a bit short. 'I'm sorry, it's just that, well, the sooner we get this job finished, the better, eh?'

'OK,' Jake agreed. 'I'll run home, check out what those words mean and come back.'

Brandon was already attacking the remaining wallpaper with the steamer again. He nodded. 'And put that picture back on your way out,' he said, gesturing to the small framed photo sticking out of Jake's pocket. Then he turned back to the mural, anxious to see the next section.

'I won't be long,' Jake said.

Brandon didn't answer him. He was too busy working. The door swung smoothly shut behind Jake with its customary little sigh, but Brandon barely heard it.

Now that he was alone in the room, Brandon's work reached a fever pitch. He steamed and scraped determinedly at the wallpaper, tearing it off and hurling it away until only half of the fourth and final wall remained covered.

Breathing hard, he worked on, inspired by the knowledge that he had nearly finished – that soon he would be able to see the mural in its entirety. He tore away two more strips of wallpaper, and staggered backwards eagerly to see what he had revealed.

It was a group of figures in Victorian dress. And in the foreground there was another figure that seemed curiously out of place – not in terms of his clothes, but because of his attitude. This time it was a young boy, his hands to his head, his face contorted in a scream.

Brandon scanned the rest of the mural, his gaze travelling slowly through the historical progression from Tudor to Victorian. He was fascinated by the figures who stared out of the painting. He had the strong feeling that they were trying to tell him something. His gaze drifted up to the Latin phrase that was constantly repeated above the picture. Was *that* what the figures were trying to tell him? He wondered how long Jake had been gone, and whether his brother had managed to translate the Latin.

He was so impatient to know what the Latin

meant that he reached for his mobile phone, intending to call Jake and see what he had learned, but then he saw that there were only three more strips of wallpaper left. Once those were removed, the entire mural would be visible. Perhaps then he would know what the strange frightened figures were trying to say. All thoughts of calling Jake were instantly forgotten.

Brandon set to work with the steamer and the putty knife, working feverishly to remove the last vestiges of the wallpaper. His breathing was shallow, his T-shirt soaked with sweat, so when he tore away two of the final strips, he took a break to look at the next part of the picture.

He found himself looking at a scene from the 1960s. At least, he guessed it was the 1960s from the look of the clothes the painted figures were wearing. As he had come to expect, the transition from the previous scene to this one was seamless. The sky was still brilliant blue, the grass emerald green. And, apart from the figures that populated the background of the scene, there was one other figure who stared out of the mural with an expression so intense and lifelike that Brandon felt she was looking directly at him.

It was a pretty young girl with her blonde hair in pigtails. And as Brandon looked at her, in spite of the heat in the room, he felt icy cold. He tried to swallow, but it felt as if someone had filled his throat with chalk.

He knew that face. He had seen the girl's features before. He felt his heart pounding against his ribs as he rushed from the room and down the stairs. He found the photograph that he was looking for in the hallway, and raced back upstairs to the mural, clutching his prize.

He held the small, framed picture of the two girls in pigtails up against the painting. And now there could be no doubt. The resemblance was just too strong. Even the clothes were the same. The little girl in the painting was identical to the one in the photograph. It was Great-aunt Lucy's missing sister.

* * *

Brandon almost dropped the photo. He looked from the picture in his hand to the painted figure on the wall and back again, but the likeness was unmistakable. He set the photo down and glanced at the last remaining strip of wallpaper.

He had to get that off. Had to see what lay beneath. His curiosity gnawed at him furiously, driving him on relentlessly as he ran the steamer over the last strip.

The last piece of wallpaper clung defiantly to the mural but, eventually, Brandon pulled the thick, crusty paper free. He hurled it to the floor and gazed at the final piece of the picture.

The mural showed a near-perfect representation of Great-aunt Lucy's house, complete with the green hills that surrounded it and the dazzling blue sky above. And, over the whole scene, appeared the same words that had been duplicated over each section of the mural from beginning to end: *Fatum tuum, nisi celata fuerit pictura, idem erit.*

However, unlike the other parts of the mural, this last section was different. There were no figures in this scene at all. Brandon frowned and moved closer, stretching out his fingertips.

In the foreground there was an unpainted area. He could see bare wall where grass should have been. And as he peered at it, he felt the hairs on the back of his neck rise once more. The weird feeling that someone was blowing softly on the back of his neck struck Brandon again. He whirled around to see if Jake had returned, but there was no one there. He was alone in the room.

Suddenly, to his left, he heard a low groaning sound. He turned back to the mural and what he saw almost caused him to scream in terror. The figure of Great-aunt Lucy's sister was moving towards him through the picture!

The painted figure grew larger as she drew nearer to the foreground of the mural and her arms reached out towards Brandon, as if she was begging for help.

No! This is impossible, Brandon thought, but he couldn't tear himself away. The girl was now life size, only slightly shorter than he was, and Brandon was sure he could make out the lines and texture of her skin, as if her hand had actually come out *through the wall*.

Brandon shook his head and blinked, convinced that his eyes and his mind must be playing tricks on him. His heart pounding, he took a step closer to the mural.

As he approached, the girl reached out further towards him, still with a pleading look on her face. In response, Brandon found himself slowly stretching out his own hand, until his fingertips touched hers.

Immediately, her hand shot forwards into the room, her fingers grasping at Brandon's arm. This time, as her fingers closed around his wrist, Brandon *did* shout out in shock and fear. Instinctively, he tried to pull his arm away, but the girl's grip was uncannily strong and he could not free himself.

He looked up from the fingers around his arm into the eyes of the girl who held him. The expression on her face had changed now, from one of pleading to one of ugly and furious determination.

This isn't happening, Brandon thought frantically. *It's some kind of bizarre illusion, caused by heat, or overwork, or* something*!*

Wasn't it?

Suddenly, the hand tugged at him, hard, pulling him towards the mural. Brandon braced himself for the collision with the wall, but it never came. Instead, he felt a terrible sucking sensation all around him, as if the wall itself was swallowing him whole.

Brandon opened his mouth to scream, but the breath was knocked from his body as he landed heavily on what felt like grass. He lay on his back for a moment, trying to catch his breath. The familiar smell of fresh-cut grass filled his nostrils and, above him, the sky was clear and blue.

Brandon struggled to his feet, his legs shaking a little, his mind still reeling from what had just happened. He quickly realized that he was standing in his great-aunt's front garden. The sun shone down upon him and he could even feel a cool breeze against his skin.

Bemusedly, Brandon walked up to the front door and knocked hard – but his fist made no sound on the wood. And there was no answer from inside. He moved along to the nearest window, cupped his hands around his eyes and peered through the murky glass. There was nothing inside. No dusty living-room with crumbling plaster and hundreds of portraits. Just a wall of darkness – as if somebody had painted the glass itself black.

Brandon looked to his right and left, becoming more terrified by the second. Beyond the house and its gardens, green fields stretched away.

'Brandon!' came Jake's voice suddenly.

As Brandon turned, his jaw dropped. Where the blue sky met the horizon, he could see the room in

Great-aunt Lucy's house that he had just left. The realization hit him like a thunderbolt: he was *inside* the painting!

Jake was coming through the door.

'Jake, over here!' Brandon yelled, desperately. 'I'm inside the painting! Help me!' But Brandon could see that Jake wasn't hearing a word he said.

'Brandon, the Latin words,' Jake called. 'They mean, "Your fate will be the same if the mural is not concealed".'

Trapped within the mural, looking out at his brother, Brandon knew how true those words actually were. He shouted Jake's name until he was hoarse, but his brother only stared blankly around the room.

'"Your fate will be the same if the mural is not concealed",' Jake mumbled again, then headed towards the door. He was about to leave when Great-aunt Lucy entered, carrying several rolls of fresh, new wallpaper and a big tub of paste.

'I brought this new wallpaper for you to put up,'

she said brightly, stepping into the room. 'What's this?' she asked, pausing as she saw the spectacular mural that now stretched around all four walls of the bedroom.

Brandon watched her gaze finally settle on a section of the painting that seemed to be to his right.

She let the rolls of wallpaper and the paste fall from her arms. 'My sister!' she exclaimed softly, her voice cracking. She took a step towards the wall. 'That's my sister, Josephine!' she screamed, and she began clawing at the wall as if trying to reach into the mural. 'Josie!'

Brandon wondered if perhaps Great-aunt Lucy would be able to hear him. 'Get me out, please!' he shrieked, watching his great-aunt scrabbling at the wall. 'Help me!'

But neither Great-aunt Lucy nor Jake seemed able to hear him at all.

Brandon saw Jake trying to pull his great-aunt away from the wall.

'Why can't you see me?' Brandon screamed from inside the mural. 'Jake, help!'

But Jake was more concerned with helping Great-aunt Lucy. 'No, no. It's just a picture. Just try to relax and calm down,' he said gently. 'Why don't you go and have a lie-down? I'll start putting up the new wallpaper.'

Great-aunt Lucy wiped her eyes with a little lace handkerchief and nodded. 'Thank you,' she whimpered. 'But the girl in the painting, she looks just like my twin sister.'

'I know,' Jake told her. 'But it's just a picture.'

Brandon raised his hands in desperation. *It's not just a picture*, he thought. 'Jake, look at me!' he tried shouting again, his throat now sore with the effort. 'Help me!'

Great-aunt Lucy moved slowly out of the room and Jake prized the lid off the tub of wallpaper paste. Then, as Brandon watched, he moved the stepladder into position and reached for a roll of the new wallpaper. Carefully, he laid it out on the floor and covered it with paste. Holding it up in front of him, Jake walked towards the mural where Brandon was imprisoned and climbed the stepladder.

'Jake, help me. Please, help me. Get me out of here. *Please!*' Brandon screamed, now sobbing with fear and desperation.

But Jake merely lifted the piece of wallpaper and prepared to smooth it into place on the wall.

'No,' pleaded Brandon from inside the mural. 'NOOOO!'

Jake pressed the paper into position and Brandon screamed again as everything around him went dark. It was as if someone had blotted out the sun.

Brandon let out one last desperate howl of despair: 'HELP ME!'

But no one did and, as he screamed helplessly inside his painted prison, Brandon knew that no one ever would.